This Isn't The Sort Of Thing That Happens To Someone Like You

Jon McGregor

BLOOMSBURY

LONDON · NEW DELHI · NEW YORK · SYDNEY

First published in Great Britain 2012
This paperback edition published 2013

Copyright © 2012 by Jon McGregor
Linocuts © 2012 by Paul Greeno

The moral right of the author has been asserted

Bloomsbury Publishing, London, New Delhi, New York and Sydney

50 Bedford Square, London WC1B 3DP

A CIP catalogue record for this book is available
from the British Library

ISBN 978 1 4088 3038 3
10 9 8 7 6 5 4 3

Typeset by Hewer Text UK Ltd, Edinburgh
Printed in Great Britain by CPI Group (UK) Ltd, Croydon CR0 4YY

MIX
Paper from
responsible sources
FSC® C020471

www.bloomsbury.com/jonmcgregor

For Éireann Lorsung,
& Matthew Welton

Contents

That Colour   3

In Winter The Sky   5

She Was Looking For This Coat   36

Looking Up Vagina   39

Keeping Watch Over The Sheep   43

Airshow   49

We Were Just Driving Around   52

If It Keeps On Raining   57

Fleeing Complexity   75

Vessel   76

Which Reminded Her, Later   82

The Chicken And The Egg   102

New York   107

French Tea   115

Close   119

We Wave And Call   130

Supplementary Notes To The Testimony   147

Thoughtful   157

The Singing   158

Wires   160

What Happened To Mr Davison   176

Years Of This, Now   182

The Remains   188

The Cleaning   193

The Last Ditch   196

Dig A Hole   214

I Remember There Was A Hill   215

Song   218

I'll Buy You A Shovel   219

Memorial Stone   253

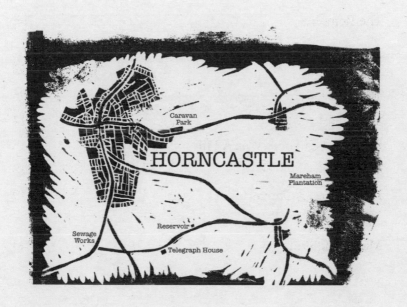

That Colour

Horncastle

She stood by the window and said, Those trees are turning that beautiful colour again. Is that right, I asked. I was at the back of the house, in the kitchen. I was doing the dishes. The water wasn't hot enough. She said, I don't know what colour you'd call it. These were the trees on the other side of the road she was talking about, across the junction. It's a wonder they do so well where they are, with the traffic. I don't know what they are. Some kind of maple or syca-more, perhaps. This happens every year and she always seems taken by surprise. These years get shorter every year. She said, I could look at them all day, I really could. I rested my hands in the water and I listened to her stand-ing there. Her breathing. She didn't say anything. She kept standing there. I emptied the bowl and refilled it with hot water. The room was cold, and the steam poured out of the water and off the dishes. I could feel it on my face. She said, They're not just red, that's not it, is it now. I rinsed off the frying pan and ran my fingers around it to check for grease. My knuckles were starting to ache again, already. She said, When you close your eyes on a sunny day, it's a bit like that colour. Her voice was very quiet. I stood still and listened. She said, It's hard to describe. A lorry went past and the whole house shook with it and I heard her step away from the window, the way she does. I asked why she was so surprised. I told her it was autumn, it was what happened: the days get shorter, the chlorophyll breaks down, the leaves turn a different colour. I told her she went through this every year. She said, It's just lovely, they're lovely, that's all, you don't have to. I finished the dishes and poured out the water and rinsed the bowl. There was a very red skirt she used to wear, when we were young. She dyed her hair to match it once and some people in the town were moved to comment. Flame-red, she called it then. Perhaps these leaves were like that, the ones she was trying to describe. I dried my hands and went through to the front room and stood beside her. I felt for her hand and held it. I said, But tell me again.

4

In Winter The Sky

Upwell

He had something to tell her. He announced this the next day, after the fog had cleared, while the floods still lay over the fields. It looked like a difficult thing for him to say. His hands were shaking. She asked him if it couldn't wait until after she'd done some work, and he said that there was always something else to do, some other reason to wait and to not talk. All right, she said. Fine. Bring the dogs. They gave his father some lunch, and they walked out together along the path beside the drainage canal.

She knew what he wanted to tell her, but she didn't know what he would say.

What she knew about him when she was seventeen: he lived at the very end of the school-bus route; he was planning to go to agricultural college when he finished his A levels; he didn't talk much; he had nice hair; he didn't have a girlfriend.

What she knew about him now: he didn't talk much; he had a bald patch which he refused to protect from the sun; he didn't read; he was a careful driver; he trimmed his toenails by hand, in bed; he often forgot to remove his boots when coming into the house; he said he still loved her.

He was seventeen the first time he kissed a girl. The girl had long dark hair, and brown eyes, and chapped lips. They sank low in their seats on the school bus, leaning together, and she took his face in her hands and pushed her mouth on to his. She seemed to know what she was doing, he said later. He was wrong. She drew away just as he was beginning to get a sense of what he'd been missing, and said that she'd like to see him again that same evening. If he wasn't busy. They should go somewhere, she said, do something. He didn't ask where, or what. She got off the bus without saying anything else, and went into her house without looking back. She ran upstairs to her bedroom, and watched the bus move slowly towards the horizon, and wrote about the boy in her notebook.

Leaving March, where she lived then, the school bus passed through Wimblington before swinging round to follow the B1098, parallel to Sixteen Foot Drain, until it stopped near Upwell. It was a journey he made every day, from the school where he was studying for his A levels to his father's house where he helped on the farm in the evenings. Where the two of them run the farm together now. The road beside the Sixteen Foot is perfectly straight, lifted just above the level of the fields, and looking out of the window that afternoon felt, he said later, in a phrase she noted down, like he was passing through the sky.

The girl's name was Joanna. The boy's name was George. He came back for her the same night.

In summer the sky is most times blue.
A blue so pure & bright ~~that~~ it hurts to look into ~~it~~ .
~~A blue~~ so deep that if you look ~~straight~~ up you ~~have to grab~~
~~something for~~ fear ~~of~~ falling

                    in.
The light ~~pouring~~ which pours from out of this blue~~ness~~ sears
everything it can reach

        / fields of wheat / canals & drains / tarmac roads /

In summer the sky is blue & lifted high
                    a shimmering blue silence from which
                    there is no hiding place
(save)   beneath the surface of the land.

                              he came back for   her
                                        the taste of

                    like he was passing through the sky

                    to go somewhere and do something

7

He has told her this part of the story many times, with the well-rehearsed air of a story being prepared for the grandchildren: how he waited until his father was asleep before taking the car-keys from the kitchen drawer, that he'd driven before, pulling trailers along farm tracks, but he didn't have a licence and his father would never have given him permission, how he remembered that she'd said she wanted to see him, to *go somewhere and do something*, that he knew he couldn't just sit there in that silent house, doing his homework and listening to the weather forecast and getting ready for bed.

She wonders, now, what would have been different if he had stayed home that night. She wants to know how he thinks he would feel, if that were the case. An impossible question, really.

The roads were empty and straight, and there was enough moonlight to steer by. She saw him coming from a long way off. Watching his headlights as they swung around the corners and pointed the way towards her. She was waiting outside by the time he got there.

She hadn't wanted to go anywhere in particular. She just wanted to sit beside him in the car and drive through the flatness of the landscape, looking down across the fields from the elevated roads. They drove from her house to Westry, over Twenty Foot Drain, past Whittlesey, and as they passed through Pondersbridge she put her hand on his thigh and kissed his ear. They crossed Forty Foot Bridge and drove through Ticks Moor, the windows open to the damp rich smell of a summer night in the fens, and beside West Moor he put his hand into her hair. They crossed the Old Bedford and New Bedford rivers, drove through Ten Mile Bank, Salter's Lode

In autumn the sky is most times white.

A ragged, dirty white.

And you wonder how this could be the same sky but it is.

The earth turns thick & hard beneath it.

Winds rip through the clouds and

slashes   of   light

run across the fields and vanish over the horizon and leave

the land as heavy as before.

The colours of the earth change.   Westry

Fields & ditches clog with leaves.   Whittlesey

Rivers swell.   Pondersbridge

Forty Foot Bridge

Ticks Moor

West Moor

Ten Mile Bank

Salter's Lode

Outwell

Friday Bridge

~~If you had stayed at home it~~
~~would never have happened.~~

We know the seasons are changing mostly by the shape & colour
of the sky.

s t r e t c h e d   o v e r   u s   f r o m
h o r i z o n   t o   h o r i z o n
t h e   l e n g t h   &   b r e a d t h   o f   a   d a y .

and Outwell, and on the edge of Friday Bridge she asked him to stop the car and they kissed for a long time.

Afterwards, they looked out across the fields and talked. They didn't know each other very well, then. He asked about her family and she asked about his. He told her about his mother, and she said she was sorry. She asked what he was going to do when he left school and he said he didn't know. He asked her the same and she said she wanted to write but that her father wanted her to go to agricultural college. She lifted his thin woollen jumper over his head and drew shapes on his bare skin with the sharp edge of her fingernail. She watched as he undid the buttons of her blouse. She took his hands and placed them against her breasts. There was the touch of her whisper in his ear, and the taste of his mouth, and the feel of his warm skin against hers, and the way his scalp moved when she pulled at his hair. Later, there was the smell of him on her hands as she stood outside her house and watched him drive away in his father's car, the two red lights getting smaller and smaller but never quite fading from view in the dark, flat land.

He drove home along the straight road beside the Sixteen Foot, holding his hand to his chest. The moonlight shining off the narrow water. He was thinking about all the things she'd said, just as she was thinking about all the things he'd said.

He was thinking about his father, he said later, and about how long his father had been alone, and about how he knew now that he wouldn't be able to live on his own in the same way. Not now he knew what it meant to be with someone else.

In winter the sky is most times grey.

A dark & bruising grey.

The days shorten.

The distance between the horizons shrinks. What little light
~~seeps down~~ is thick & lifeless.

~~In winter there's~~ no danger of falling into the sky
~~Our bodies~~ anchored to the ground by the weight of the light.

The earth hides secrets.

The land is silent.

The drains & canals will freeze and be covered in snow.

The snow will come fast in the night and
block the roads & drains and leave
nothing
but whiteness
(all lines & textures concealed).

The land giving back light to the sky.

He was still thinking about her when he drove into a man and killed him.

First he was driving along the empty road thinking about her, and then there was a man in the road looking over his shoulder and the car was driving into him. It was hard to know where he'd come from. He'd come from nowhere. He was not there and then he was there and there was no time to do anything. There was no time to flinch, or to shout. He didn't even have time to move his hand from his chest, and as the car hit the man he was flung forwards and his hand was crushed against the steering wheel. The man's arms lifted up to the sky and his back arched over the bonnet and his legs slid under one of the wheels and his whole body was dragged down to the road and out of sight.

Those arms lifted up to the sky, that arching back.

The sound the man's body made when the car struck him. It was too loud, too firm, it sounded like a car driving into a fence rather than a man. And the sound he made. That muffled split-second of calling-out.

His arms lifted up to the sky, even his fingers pointing upwards, as if there was something he could reach up there to pull himself clear. His back arching over the bonnet of the car before being dragged down. The jolt as he was lost beneath the wheels. George's hand crushed between his chest and the steering wheel.

Then stillness and quiet.

He lay on his back with his legs underneath him, looking up at the night. His legs were bent back so far that they must have been broken. George stood by the car for a long time. The man didn't make a sound. There was no sound

In spring the sky is all these colours. Spring comes

                                         gradually here.

Broad beans & early wheat break through the surface of the soil.

Pale green buds squeeze out from dry branches

while the sky fades to light grey & white & ~~finally a~~ faint blue.

The air ~~cleanses itself~~ is cleansed, ~~with~~ by

a warm wind from the south

bursts of sparkling rain

The sky lifts away from the ground.   those arms lifted

                                         up to the sky.

The horizons draw apart

and stretch the sky taut and

space & light flood back into our lives.

                                      that arching back.

This is the time when change

is a daily force:

                  woodlands smeared green overnight

                  fields purpled with lavender behind your back

                  ~~wives & mothers & daughters pregnant by dawn~~

This is the time when the floods come

and the ditches and barriers have to be built again,

~~a little~~ deeper

~~a little~~ higher

But still, with all this life bursting up towards the sky,

                              (the earth holds secrets)

                              (the sky watches)

The hills having eyes means nothing here.

The land is level and all we have watching over us is the sky.

anywhere. The night was quiet and the moon bright and the air still and there was a man lying in the road a few yards away. It didn't feel real, and there were times now when they both wondered whether it had really happened at all. But there was the way the man's neck felt when George touched his fingers against the vein there. Not cold, but not warm either, not warm enough: *he feels like a still-born calf*. There was no pulse to feel. Only his broken body on the tarmac, his eyes, his open mouth.

He was wearing a white shirt, a red V-necked jumper, a frayed tweed jacket. His arms were up beside his head, and his fists were tightly clenched. A broken half-bottle of whisky was hanging from the pocket of his jacket. There didn't seem to be any blood anywhere; there were dirty black bruises on his face, which might have been old bruises anyway, but there was no blood. His clothes were ripped across the chest, but there was no blood. It was hard to understand how a man could be *dragged under the wheels of a car and not bleed*. It was hard to understand how he could not bleed and yet die so quickly.

The whites of his eyes looked yellow under the moonlight.

It was hard to understand who he was, and why he had been on the road in the middle of the night. Why he was dead now. It was hard to know what to do. George knelt beside him, looking out across the fields, up at the sky, at his father's car, his shaking hands, the sky.

~~This place I've grown up in is~~ a landscape of lines,
~~a world of~~ the parallel & perpendicular.
~~The straightest line of all is the~~ hard blur of the horizon.

....

A single unbending line which encircles the day.

....

~~When I was~~ As a child I would spin around
~~with my eyes on the horizon~~ trying to catch the place where
the line turned or bent   but I never could

the mystery of the straight, encircling line.

-      -   -   -   -   -   -   -

(All the) other lines find their way to the horizon ~~sooner or later~~

High lines,   (Years ago, playing in the
connecting lines: telegraph wires   furrows while your father
                  railway tracks   watched, you looked up +
                  canals   saw a line of boats gliding
                  drains   through the sky. The fear
                  rivers   you felt, seeing those
                                         boats above your head.)

Low lines,
boundary lines: ditches   (No hedges or walls
                roads   between fields here,
                paths   only the ditches + roads.
                                         Ditches to stop the sea
                                         reclaiming what it owns.)

He had his reasons, he says. He's often regretted it, and he's often thought that his reasons weren't enough, but he thinks he would do the same again.

If he'd been older when he made that journey then perhaps he would have been stronger; perhaps his thoughts would have been clearer. But he was seventeen, and he had never knelt beside a dead man before. So he drove away. He stood up, and turned away from the man, and walked back to his father's car, and drove away. He didn't look in the rear-view mirror, and he didn't turn around when he slowed for the junction.

I suppose it was at that stage that I began to realise ~~what had happened~~ *what I had done.*

That was how he put it, when he told her, walking out on the path beside the canal after lunch, the dogs running along ahead of them with their claws clicking on the tarmac strip. *I suppose.*

He had driven his father's car into a man, and then over him, and now that man was dead. He felt a sort of sickness, a watery dread, starting somewhere down in his guts and rising to the back of his throat. His hands were locked on the wheel. He couldn't even blink.

And he knew, even before he got back to his father's house, that he would have to return to the man. He couldn't leave him laid out on the road like that, with his legs neatly folded under his back. He knew, or he thought he knew, that when the man was found then somehow he would be found too, and the girl who'd drawn upon his bare chest wouldn't even look him in the eye.

So it was her fault as well, it seems.

16

The lines of this place are sometimes washed out by floods.
Obliteration.
Water erasing the   (Cornelius the Dutchman
manmade geometry   digging his way through
restoring this place   the 17th century.)
to the sea it once was.

Sometimes it will be rain, swelling the rivers until they break
through
and rush over the fields,
settling across hundreds of acres for weeks at a time,
sky below as well as above, clouds & seabirds gliding overhead
sky above as well as below, clouds & seabirds gliding overland.

Or snow will cover everything, blocking drains & roads,
....
Mothers forbidding their children to leave the house.
Lost children in the fields.
~~You said you don't remember your mother telling you to go out,~~
~~but you would have been too young to remember/to go out.~~
Sometimes   the   fog
                                       will
        come   in   with
                the
floods   and
                        our   world
        will
                become
unmappable,   alien,
                        precarious.
————————————   ~~I didn't say you said it was my fault~~

17

He fetched a shovel from a barn at his father's farm and drove back to where he'd hit the man. *It sounds so terrible now.* Cowardly? He carried the shovel down the embankment to the field below the road and took off his jumper and began to dig.

He was used to digging. *The field had only recently been harvested, and the stubble was still in the ground*, so he lay sections of topsoil to one side to be replaced. He was thinking clearly, working quickly but properly, ignoring the purpose of the hole. Once, *knee-deep in the ground*, he looked up the bank and realised what he was doing. But he couldn't see the man up on the road, so he managed to swallow the rising sickness and dig some more. And all this time, the sound of metal on soil, the sky above.

And then it was deep enough. It was done. So long as it was *further beneath the surface than the plough-blades would reach then it was deep enough, most probably*. He climbed up the embankment to the road, wanting to hurry and get it done but holding back from what he had to do, from the fact of *having to touch him, having to pick him up* and carry him down the bank and into the hole he had made. The death he had made in the hole he had made in the earth. He bent down to take the man's arms. He *could smell whisky*. He stopped, unwilling to touch him, unwilling to go through with what he'd found reason to do. *They were good reasons, but they didn't seem enough*. But then he remembered her skin on his, and her eyes, and he knew, he said, that he *could do anything not to lose that*.

She'd made him do it, then. That was how it had happened.

These same floods ~~that obliterate~~ bring life to the land, make

                                               our soil the richest in the country.

At ploughing time the smell of the earth hangs in the air,

a smell like apple bruises and horse chestnut shells.

                                          A smell of pure energy.

Your father claimed this ground

would grow five-pound notes

if you planted a shilling.

                                          That I would like to see.

Flatness | straight lines | a manmade geometry.

The sound of metal on soil   //   the sky above

This is the landscape ~~you I~~ we grew up in.

This is the landscape ~~which grew us~~ which made us.

The sea wants to be here. ~~we shouldn't be surprised when~~

                    will give   to that

Our engineering   ~~gives~~   way ~~before the sea's~~ desire.

                              ~~You didn't say that. That's not what you said~~

He gripped the man's elbows and lifted them up to his waist. He backed away towards the embankment and the man's legs unfolded from beneath him, his head rolling down into his armpit, his *half-bottle of whisky falling from his pocket* and breaking on the road. He didn't stop. He kept dragging him away, *away from the road, down the bank, into the field.*

She'd said, when he finally told her all this, that she wanted to know it all. How it was done. How it had felt. So now she knew.

He laid the man down beside the hole in the earth and rolled him into it. The man fell face down, and he *felt bad about that*, about the man's face being in the mud. He went back to the place on the road and picked up the pieces of glass. He threw them down on to the man's back, and then he took the shovel and began to *pile the earth back into the hole.*

He threw soil over the man until he was gone, until the soil pressed down on him so that he was no longer a man or a body or a victim or anything. Just an absence, hidden under the ground. It was only then that he looked up at the sky, dark and silent over him, the moon hidden by a cloud. He drove past her house in March again, and then back to his father's house. He put the car-keys away in the kitchen drawer, and the shovel in the barn, and he stood in the shower until the hot-water tank had emptied and he was left standing beneath a trickle of water as cold as stone.

So now she knew.

                    to name these places

The words we've been given ~~by our ancestors~~ have no poetry.

Our waterways are called drains,

not rivers or streams or brooks or burns:

	Thirty Foot Drain
	Sixteen Foot Drain
(and the closest to grandeur, this)	Hundred Foot Drain
our farms named for anonymity:	Lower Field Farm
	Middle Field Farm
	Sixteen Foot Farm

~~People don't come here because they've been~~

People are not drawn here by the romantic sound of the place.

People don't much come here at all, and so the landscape

remains empty and

retains its beauty and

the beauty of this place is not in the names but the shapes

the flatness / hugeness / completeness of the landscape.

Only what is beneath the surface of the earth is hidden

~~(and sometimes not even that)~~

~~and~~ everything else ~~is~~ made visible beneath the sky.

They were married before either of them had the chance to go to university: his father retired early, after a heart attack, and he had to take over the farm. It only made sense for Joanna to move in and help. George had been there when his father collapsed: he'd heard the dogs barking at the tractor in the yard, and gone outside to see his father clutching at his chest and turning pale. He'd dragged him from the cab into the mud and begun hammering on his chest. *I didn't want to lose him to the land as well*. He'd beaten his father's heart with his fist, and forced air into his lungs, and called out for help. She was there with him. She rang the ambulance, and watched him save his father's life, and decided she would marry him. She can remember very clearly, standing there and deciding that. And he still thinks he was the one who asked her.

When she remembers it now, it's always from a height, as if she can see it the way the sky saw it: George kneeling over his father in the mud of the yard, shouting at him to hold on, the dogs circling and barking.

And now this giant of a man sits in an armchair clutching a hot-water bottle and watching the sky change colour outside. He refuses to watch television, listening instead to the radio while he keeps watch on the land and the sky. He claims to take no interest in the running of the farm: he signed everything over to them almost immediately, and has rarely offered an opinion. But she knows that he watches. She has seen him looking at a newly ploughed field from the upstairs window, or running a hand along a piece of machinery in the yard, or lingering by the kitchen table while she does the accounts. She has seen the faint

22

When the dawn comes

~~when the first light slides in from the east~~

the sky is the colour of marbles.

                                    A thin, glassy grey.

Everything is dark away to the west,

silhouettes & shadows clinging to the last of the night,

but at the eastern ~~edge of the~~ horizon there is light.

~~And~~ If you have the time to stand and watch,

you can trace the movement of the light into the morning.

The lines of fields & roads creeping

towards you and then away to the west

until the ~~whole~~ geometry of the day is revealed.

~~And~~ The water in the drains begins to steam & shine.

~~And you'll notice~~ The workers start to arrive,

stepping out from minibuses and spreading across the fields,

shadows crouching & shuffling

along the ~~crop-lines~~ lines of the crops.

smiles and nods which indicate that he is well pleased. She hopes that George has noticed; she suspects that he has not. Sometimes, when George takes his father his evening meal, his father will talk about something he's heard on the radio: a concert recording, a weather forecast, a news report. Often they'll just sit, and George will listen to his father's short creaking breaths, thankful to have him there still. She doesn't sit with them at these times. She reads, or deals with paperwork, or goes back to her writing, waiting for him to reassure himself that his father is well.

They've never had children, ~~and this has~~
~~They've never talked about it, and yet~~

In this way, their lives together had settled into something like a routine. He was up first, feeding the dogs, bringing her a cup of tea, eating his breakfast and leaving his dishes on the table. She dressed, and ate her breakfast, and cleared the table, and waited until she heard the radio in his father's bedroom before going to help him dress.

Caring for his father had taken up more and more of their time over the years. His health was poor enough to justify moving him into a nursing home. There was one over in March; she had a friend whose mother was there, and had heard good reports. But it was obvious that his father would refuse to go. And she had been unable to find a way of bringing it up with George. There were so many things she was unable to bring up with him. Sometimes it felt as though they only related to each other through talking about work, about *the business*. As business partners, they have been close, communicative, collaborative. All those good words.

When the mid-morning comes
the sky is the colour of flowering linseed

a pale-blue hint of
the full colour to come

Sometimes there will be clouds, ~~joining together to form arches~~
~~from horizon~~ ~~to~~ ~~horizon~~
stretching
tearing
scattering patterns across the fields.

Sometimes these clouds bring rain,

and the sky will darken
But the rain will pass
the sky be brighter   clearer

The workers more visible,
returning to their trays & boxes after the rain,
lifting food from the ground,
sorting
trimming
laying down
moving along the line.

Occasionally one will stand, lifting cramped arms to the sky before
returning to the soil.

~~Those lifted arms, that arching back.~~

25

~~In the mornings and the afternoons, they worked in the~~ ~~fields.~~ That wasn't really true. It might have been true once, in the very early days, when they'd had to work hard all the hours of daylight to try and pull the business out of the hole his father had dug it into. There'd been no money to employ extra labour, and they'd had to do everything themselves. There was less land then, but it was still a struggle and they were always exhausted by the time they found their way to bed.

But things had changed, gradually. They'd bought more land, secured more grants and loans. *Diversified*. And almost without noticing, they'd stopped being farmers and become managers. Most of the field-work was done by labourers hired by sub-contractors, people they never spoke to. George still liked to do some of the work himself – the ploughing, the ditch-digging, the heavy machine-based jobs – but there was no real need. For the most part they spent their days on the phone, or filling out forms, buying supplies, dealing with inspectors, negotiating with the water authorities. Discussions about drainage and flood defences seemed to take more and more of her time now. The floods seemed to be coming more often, covering more land, taking longer to drain. *Maybe we should switch to rice*, George had started saying, and she wasn't sure whether or not this was a joke.

All of which meant that when he said he wanted to tell her something, and that they should take the time to walk out along the path beside the canal after lunch, it was no real interruption to the running of the farm. Down in the few

When the noon-time comes

    (when there's a moment of stillness and silence)

the sky is the colour of the summer noon:

    a blue with no comparison

        the pure deep blue of the summer noon in this place.

No clouds

no movement

you hold your breath and turn and follow the circle of the

~~unbending horizon line~~   horizon's circle.

The workers eat their lunch in silence, gathered beside the road,

looking out across the fields

the way fishermen watch the sea.

Celery &

spring onions &

leeks &

lettuces &

fragile crops which would be ruined by machinery.

fields which weren't yet flooded, the workers carried on, their backs bent low, and she was able to stop him and put her hand to his chest and ask what it was he wanted to say.

In the evenings he often spent time in the barn, fixing things. She would spend that time walking backwards and forwards from the house to the barn, offering to help, and having that help warmly but firmly rejected. He was unable to admit, even now, that she was better than he was at mechanical jobs: repair, maintenance, improvised alteration and the like. Her father had been a mechanic. It was natural that she would have an ability in that area. But still, he found it difficult to accept.

At the same time, he found it difficult to have sufficient patience with, or tolerance of, the writing she did. She had only ever called it writing: he was the one who used the word 'poems'. But whenever he said it – 'poems' – it was with an affected air, as if the pretension was hers. So, for example, he might come crashing in from the barn late one afternoon, with his boots on, and say *Would you just leave your bloody poems alone for one minute and help me get the seed-drill loaded up?* There were five other places he could have put the *bloody* in that sentence, but he chose to put it there, next to 'poems'. This is an example, she would tell him, if he was interested, of what placement could do.

Once, he says, he saw a man metal-detecting in that field. He was driving past and saw a car parked on the verge, a faint line of footprints leading out across the soil. The light was clear and strong, and the man in the field was no more than a silhouette. He sat in his car, watching. Twice he saw the man stoop to the ground and dig with a small shovel.

When the late afternoon comes

    (when the light is only beginning to ~~fade from the day~~ fall)

the sky is the colour of a freshly forming bruise.

The workers are slowing their pace

pausing ~~more frequently~~ to savour

the warmth of the soil in their hands

aware ~~now~~ of the slight chill in the air

                                       waiting

for the word that the day is over.

-   -   -   -   -   -   -   -   -   -   -   -

                                  What placement can do.

-   -   -   -   -   -   -   -   -   -   -   -

When the evening comes

    (before the embers of the closing of the day)

the sky is the colour of your father's eyes.

A darkening, muddied blue,

hiding shadows

    turning away.   Awake, still;

                                   alive, just;

                                   but going.

                                   Going gently.

The workers have left the field and collected their pay,

measured by the weight of the food they have gathered.

The marks of their footprints are fading,

dusted over with soil blown in by a wind from the sea.

29

Twice he *saw him stand and kick the earth back into place*, and continue his steady sweeping with the metal detector. He wanted to go and tell him to stop, but there was no good reason for doing so. It wasn't his land. *The man would surely have asked permission, and anyway he was doing no damage so soon after harvest.*

He wondered what the man thought he was going to find, he says. He had a sudden feeling of inevitability; that this would be the moment when the body was found, the moment when everything could be made right. He thought about going to fetch Joanna, so she could be there to see it as well.

He'd been living like this for years, it would seem, lurching between a trembling silence and a barely withheld confessional urge. When he thought about it later, he realised there was no reason why a man with a metal detector should find a body. But *that kind of logical thought* seemed to crumble in the face of these moments.

He got out of the car, and waited. The man in the field looked up at George, and George looked down at him. Ready. The man packed his tools into a bag and began hurrying back to his car, stumbling slightly across the low stubble.

Did you find anything? George asked.

No, the man said, nothing. And he got in his car and drove away.

                                        What he thought he'd find.

There is no history here.

No dramatic finds of Saxon villages.
No burial mounds or hidden treasures.
~~No Tollund Man.~~
Only the rusted anchors our ploughs drag up,
left when these fields were the sea.

Those rusted anchors have been sunk in the soil
~~ever~~ since before it was drained,   and sometimes
the turning of the earth brings them closer to the surface

                                        and sometimes
it ~~will~~ sends them further down.

Buried out there at the edge of the field.~~Butyouwerethere~~

The sound of plough metal on soil, the roar
                                        of stones & earth.

~~As he/it~~ Tumbles further down or is hauled to the surface.

break the flat surface

This is the way it happens, in the end. This is the way he describes it, when he tells her:

He was driving, he said. There were *bright lights, and men in white overalls standing in the water*. There were police officers along the embankment and a white tent on the verge. There were police vans in the road. A policeman was directing the traffic through from either direction. *The men in white overalls were doing something with poles and tape*. He could *hardly breathe*, he said. There was *something like a rushing sound in his ears*.

The policeman waved at him to stop, and walked over to the car, and asked George to wind the window down. He reminded George that they were at school together, and George *didn't know what to say*. A funny do this, isn't it, the policeman said. George *thought the policeman was probably waiting for him to ask what had happened* but he didn't say anything. The policeman told him anyway: they'd found a body in the water. The farmer had seen it. They were assuming it had been buried for years, and that the flood water must have disturbed the soil and brought it out. There wasn't much left of it now. The policeman said he couldn't imagine they'd find out who it was, and then he asked after the family and said he should let George get on. George said that his wife and his father were both fine and drove slowly into the fog.

Later, he drove into the yard and the dogs came barking out to meet him. He sat in the car for a moment, too weak to open the door. Joanna could see him from the kitchen window. She stood and watched. She wondered what was

That field. In that field. Down by that field.

The floods have come, again,
        the road like a causeway
                across the sea.

T h e w a t e r s t r e t c h e d a s f a r a s t h e h o r i z o n
t h e

                                   h o r i z o n

      l o s t

              i n   t h e

t h i c k

                 f o g.

Telegraph	poles	dotted
across	the	water
like	the	masts
of	sunken	boats.

The cars marooned.   High & dry.
Piercing red lights suspended in a long line through the fog.

33

wrong. The lights of the house were clear and warm, spilling into the foggy night. He got out of the car and walked to the house, pushing the dogs away, and she came to meet him in the hallway. He looked at her and said that they needed to talk. She said it would have to wait until she'd finished some more work, and he said there was always something else to do, some other reason to wait and to not talk. He said they couldn't go on like this, it had gone on for too long, they were young when it happened, they were older now, time had passed, they needed to bring things out into the open and deal with the consequences and stop trying to hide what it was doing to them both. She looked at him. It was the most she had heard him say for a long time. It didn't fit. All right, she said. Fine. Bring the dogs.

He served the meal she had prepared for his father and took it through to him.

They found a body in the field down the road, his father said.

George nodded, and said that he'd heard.

Can't think it was anyone from round here, his father said.

No, George said. I shouldn't think so.

The mists of yesterday have disappeared,

       the sky reflected clearly in the flooded fields

       the sky reflected clearly in the flooded fields.

The day is broken   open & clear:

       the great ship of Ely Cathedral
       just visible
       across the water.

And we were there.

She Was Looking For This Coat

Lincoln

She came in and she was looking for this coat. It was her father's, she said. He'd left it on a bus last week. She spent a long time describing it. Herringbone was a word she used. Also she said it was a kind of faded moss-green. Or more like a faded sage-green, but like a faded *dark* sage-green, with a brown hue. She asked me if I knew the colour she meant. I said I thought I was getting the idea. She had her hands resting on the counter, and she was trying to look round behind me, the way people do, like they think I'm hiding something. She said the buttons were tortoiseshell and one of them was missing. She said the lining was a very dark navy-blue and it was torn from one of the arms right down to the hem. She asked me if I thought hem was the right word to use about a man's coat. I said I wouldn't know about that. He'd left it on a bus the previous week, she told me again, on the Wednesday. It did have a belt but that might be missing, she said. I turned the pad of

Mis/Prop/B forms across the counter towards her and asked her to fill in her name and address and telephone number. I said I could do the rest. I said I didn't think we had anything right here in the office but I could make enquiries. She was looking at the form like she couldn't read it. She said it was definitely Wednesday. She said she thought the coat was from Burton's. I asked her if she knew which bus the item had been mislaid upon. She said she didn't. She said it would have been some time in the morning. She said her father had told her he'd gone to meet his friend for lunch, when she'd spoken to him, when she'd spoken to him on the phone, last Wednesday. The way she was talking, I felt like asking her if she needed to sit down. I asked if her father had a bus pass and she nodded and I told her in that case he was unlikely to have been on the bus before nine thirty. She looked surprised. I said so we're narrowing it down now aren't we, love? I tried a smile. She didn't smile. I asked if there were any valuables in the pockets. She said she wasn't sure. She picked up the pen. She said there'll be pens in the top pocket, in the breast pocket. She started to fill in her name and address. Kathryn something. With a Y. It was a nice name. It suited her. She had very dark black hair. I told her if she could put all her contact details on the form I'd be able to make enquiries and someone would be in touch. I told her she'd given a very good description and I was sure if the coat had been handed in we'd be able to locate it for her father. There was another customer waiting by then. There's never normally another customer. I said someone would be in contact as soon as possible, if it had been handed in. I told her unfortunately in this day and age etc. She asked me had she mentioned it being a long coat. I told her I thought I'd assumed that. It came down to here on him, she said, pointing to her knees, but he was a lot taller than me so it would look longer than that on me. I started to say something but I didn't say anything. We had quite a queue by then. We never normally have a queue. I said I hoped we'd be able to locate the item for her. I told her someone would be in touch. She told me the collar was brown. She was trying to remember the name of the material. She said what's it called, it's like inside-out leather, you have to brush it, it's soft to the touch, it smells like leather but it's soft to the touch when you stroke it, it leaves marks if you stroke it the wrong way. I asked her did she mean suede and she said yes, that was it, suede. I wrote on the form that the coat had a brown suede collar. I asked her was there anything else I could help her with today.

Looking Up Vagina

Welton

He was the first boy in his class to get pubic hair. He'd vaguely assumed that this might be something the other boys would be envious of. Perhaps even awestruck by. Something which would make them see him in a new light. But it turned out to be just one more thing they could use in their campaign of vilification against him.

Vilification was a word he'd come across recently. It was a word he'd found easy to understand.

Virile was another word. It was something to do with sex. He knew pubic hairs were the first step on the way to getting sex, so he thought this might mean he was virile and the other boys would be impressed or maybe even intimidated or at the very least would reconsider their apparently venal opinions of him.

He'd had the pubic hairs for over a year now. He was used to them, and had almost forgotten that they might be an issue. The subject had never come up. But this

was the last year of primary school, and they were starting weekly swimming lessons, and at the swimming
pool there was a communal changing room. One of the
boys saw, and pointed it out to the other boys, and soon
enough all of them were looking and asking him questions about it.

And for a moment everything seemed to hang in the
balance, like when a bus hangs off the edge of a cliff and
everything depends on whether the passengers rush to
the front or the back. It would only have taken one boy
to say something like, 'cool,' or, 'nice one, Smithy,' and
everything would have been different. There might even
have been some quiet veneration, before everyone put
on their trunks and got into the pool. Word would have
spread around the school, and he would no longer have
been vulnerable to being tripped in the corridors. People
would have talked to him on the bus, or between lessons.
But instead, someone pushed the balance the other way.
Robin was in the vanguard. He shouted something,
pointing at the pubic hairs and turning to the other boys
for support. They all joined in, and the shouting continued for the rest of the day, and for some days after that.
Weeks.

'Bush' was the word that got shouted. Bush, and its
many variations, with everyone trying to think of a new
version: bush, bushy, bushwhacker, bushmonkey, bushman, bushy bushman, busharama, bushface, bush-
muppet, bushalicious, bushbum, bushbunny, busher,
bushayre, busherara, busheba, lord bush, president bush,
sir bushwhacker of bushingdon, bushmonster, bushbilly,

bushwilly, bushknocker, bushiel-san, bushelman, busha-lackalonglong, bushy-bushy-bush-bush.

It wasn't even as if his pubic hair was unusually verdant.

Someone told the girls, and so then all the girls knew that he was the first boy in the class to get pubic hair. One of them came up at lunch-time and asked him if it was true. She looked like she was on the verge of being impressed, but her friends were laughing so he said it wasn't. He said he vigorously disputed it. Robin and another boy heard this, and pulled his trousers down in order to publicly verify the facts. There was a certain amount of vicarious laughter from just about everyone in the vicinity.

He stayed home from school for a few days after that. Mostly he lay in bed, looking up vagina and vulva in the dictionary.

He understood, already, that in a few years' time these same boys would get, or claim to be getting, sex, and that he would be mocked and called a virgin. Virginal. Someone would realise that virginal sounded like vaginal, and he would be called a vagina; a vagina-head. He could visualise it precisely. There was no logic to it. It was vindictive. There was no way he could win. There wasn't really any hope of winning. It made him feel vexated.

But he also understood that one day he would leave. Eventually, he would leave. And when he was gone they would still be here. He would move to a big city, and go to university, and be friends with people who didn't feel the need to mock and belittle him, people who were interested in reading and art and philosophy and those varieties of things. And Robin and everyone else would all still be here, with their limited vocabularies, working in the chicken-processing factories and vegetable packing-houses, looking for someone else to victimise.

Victorious would be a word he could use then. Vindicated.

Keeping Watch Over The Sheep

Alford

They told him he wasn't allowed on the school premises. They didn't even use the word allowed to start off with, they just said they thought it would be better if he didn't come in. Better for everyone concerned is what they said. Only that didn't even feel like an everyone which included him. He wasn't really bothered what they thought, he said, he just wanted to come in and see his daughter. That's when they actually stepped in his way and said he literally wasn't allowed on the premises.

For Christ's sake, this was the school nativity.

When would he get another chance to come and see his little girl in her first ever school nativity? Never is when. But the man just stood there all immovable and what have you, his arms folded to show just how totally immovable he was. Said his name was Carson. *Mr* Carson. Wasn't even the headteacher or anything, but the other teachers were obviously all women so he must have been sent out to deal with the situation.

That's what he was now. A situation.

He said to Mr Carson, he said, look, it's only the school hall we're talking about here. He was only going to stand at the back. He wouldn't try and talk to her. Rachel wouldn't even have to know he was there, he could hide behind another parent, he could slip out before the end. There didn't need to be a problem here, he said. Mr Carson just stood there and said it was out of his hands.

Yeah I'll take it out of your hands you four-eyed fucking twat.

He didn't say that. He knew better than saying something like that, these days. He wasn't there to make trouble. He was just there to see a nativity play. The shepherds were mightily afraid. The wise men followed yonder bright star in the east. All that. There weren't no room at the inn. He held up his hands in surrender. A conciliatory gesture. He'd been learning about those, at the sessions. He even attempted a smile. He told Mr Carson, he said, okay, he was leaving now, he was sorry to have caused any disturbance, he hoped the performance went well and could someone perhaps tell Rachel that her father had said hello? Mr Carson did this disappointed shrug and said for him to take care. Not saying whether he would or he wouldn't pass on the hello to Rachel, take note. There were other parents hanging back behind him, waiting to get in the school, not wanting to get involved. But standing just about close enough to hear what was going on, and then none of them meeting his eye when he turned and walked away. Like they didn't know him or they didn't know what was going on.

They knew though. They all did, round here. Some of them had even known certain things before he had, when it would have been useful for him to have been told. They all like to hear stuff but they're none of them that keen on passing it on.

He got to the corner before he looked back. The other parents were all safely inside, and Mr Carson was closing the door. Bolting it, probably. Even saying something about how they couldn't be too careful. He walked off. Calmly. He followed the line of hedging around the edge of the school playing field, where the road dipped down a bit and you could see out past the edge of the village. Someone was out ploughing, which seemed early but what did he know. The seagulls were following behind the plough. He got to the sign that said *School Property: No Dog Walking*, and climbed over the double-gate there. That was harder than it used to be. Used to come over this way when he was a kid and they were looking for somewhere to play football. Or, later, for somewhere to drink. He even came over here with her once or twice, before he'd got a car.

He didn't really even have a plan, now.

He wasn't here to make trouble.

He could just stand outside the hall and listen. Rachel had such a good voice he'd probably be able to hear her over all the others. She got that from her mother, the voice. Among other things. He walked across the playing field towards the hall. Walking calmly and casually, not running or ducking down or any of that. He wasn't going to attract attention to himself. The curtains were closed, so no one could even see him. He listened right up to the glass. They were singing a song about the angels, and then when it went quiet he heard a little girl saying Joseph Joseph you must find somewhere for us to stay the baby is coming soon. That didn't sound like Rachel. Probably an older girl would be playing the part of Mary. Maybe Rachel would do it another year, when she was older. There would be other years, after all. There wouldn't always be this situation. But this was her first nativity. He couldn't miss the first one.

He didn't even know what part she was playing. He didn't know anything about it at all. He'd only found out it was on when he'd heard some women talking about it in the post office.

He didn't know if Rachel's mother would be in there. She'd have a prime seat at the front, if she was. Guaranteed. He hadn't seen her going in the whole time he'd been waiting up the road from the main entrance. But she'd got pretty good at sneaking around in the last few months. Since the injunction. So she could have easily found another way to get in. And she wouldn't be hiding behind another parent, or tucked away at the back of the hall. She'd be right in Rachel's line of sight, right where she could see her. And little Rachel would be delighted to see her, her little face would be all lighting up right now probably, in the middle of this song about the happy sheep coming down from the hills to find the baby Jesus lying in a manger, and that was fine, that was good, he was happy to think of her little face all lighting up the way it does. He just wanted to be there to see it sometimes, was all. He wanted to be the one who her little face would be lighting up about, sometimes, was all.

He saw Mr Carson coming across the field towards him, looking all purposeful and what have you. There were some others with him. He turned back towards the hall, sliding his face along the window to try and find a gap in the curtains, listening out for the sound of that one little voice he'd come to hear.

He didn't even know how it had all started going wrong. With Rachel's mother. He couldn't really blame her, not like most of the others who went to the sessions had someone to blame. It wasn't her fault. But it wasn't really his fault either, and something like that didn't just come up out of nowhere. Maybe it was both of their faults in a way. Maybe there were some things he probably shouldn't have said, or done. Or broken. Breaking things had never helped. But just sometimes it was hard to know what else to do. When she said those things. When she purposefully misunderstood what he was trying to say.

He'd always made sure Rachel wasn't there to see. That was one thing that could be said in his defence.

It was one way of getting to touch her again anyway at least.

Later, once the police had got the handcuffs on and were picking him up off the ground, he noticed that someone had opened the hall curtains, and he thought he could see Rachel standing on the edge of the stage wearing what must have been a sheep costume. She'd grown a bit since the last time he'd seen her. It didn't take long. He tried to smile at her and call hello. But unless she was doing some very good acting she was looking pretty upset, pretty tearful and scared and what have you. Which made him wonder what was going on in there, if she'd maybe been pushed into doing the school nativity when she didn't really want to, or if she'd forgotten her words and no one had helped her remember them. He wondered why no one was looking after her right now, while she was standing there on her own all tearful and upset-looking. He wondered what kind of a school this was that her mother was sending her to anyway.

He'd definitely be coming back for some answers. There wasn't any doubt about that. Just as soon as he'd sorted out this current situation. They didn't need to worry about that, any of them. He'd be coming back, and someone was going to be asked, in no uncertain terms, to explain.

Airshow

Scampton

On the long drive back from the funeral, they took the grandfather to see the airfield where he'd been stationed during the war. They thought this was something he might like to do. They parked on a grass verge beside one of the exit gates in the perimeter fence, and helped the grandfather from the car. The ground was so flat it was difficult to see anything at all. It seemed to curve away from them. They looked at him looking through the fence. The wind was blowing in from the east, and the long grass near the fence dipped and swayed with a sound like a low shush. They looked at him looking at the runway and the hangars and the other low buildings in the distance. They couldn't really see much from where they were. They waited for him to tell them something, but he seemed at a loss. He lifted a finger, as though to point something out, and withdrew it. They walked along the verge for a short distance. The grandfather wasn't much inclined to talk about the place, it seemed. Instead, he talked about living in digs in the next village along, with his new wife and their baby, and about how his wife had only ever been able to walk along the road and back because the fields and woods were too muddy for a pram. The wind picked up. It got colder. They climbed back into the car and drove south.

Later, they learned that the grandfather had worked as an armourer, loading munitions into the heavy bomber aircraft and cleaning out the gun-turrets and bomb-bays when the aircraft returned. The task would at times have involved the removal of bodies and body-parts, but that was never discussed. From this airfield, squadrons had flown out to destroy whole towns; burying households beneath rubble, igniting crematorial fires, busting dams and drowning entire valleys. Some civilians were killed. The war was won.

On their way home, they passed the modern RAF base at Coningsby, driving alongside the perimeter fence for a mile or two before entering the town itself. As they passed the end of the main runway, they saw a small gravelled car-park on the other side of the road, sheltered from the wind on three sides by a thick line of gorse bushes. The car-park was full. People were sitting beside their cars in ones and twos, on folding chairs, with blankets across their knees and thermos flasks cradled in their laps. They had binoculars and long-lensed cameras and notebooks. They were waiting for the modern fighter aircraft stationed at the base to take off and land, so that they could take pictures and make notes and gaze in awe. They were also waiting for something called 'The Memorial Flight': a regular display by vintage bomber aircraft. As though vintage was a word which could be used about a bomber plane in the same way it could be used about a car, or a suit, or a set of buttons.

As they drove past, the grandfather turned to look at the people in the car-park. He didn't say anything. He watched them through the back window. He didn't say anything as they drove through Coningsby, past the church and over the river and out along the main road to the motorway. He waited until they got back to the house, and as they helped him out of the car he asked just what it was those people with the binoculars had thought they might be waiting to see.

We Were Just Driving Around

North Ormsby

We were just driving around.

It was late in the evening but it was still light. We'd been out for hours and it was one of those nights when it seemed like basically it was never going to get dark. We hadn't seen anyone around, and a couple of times when we'd stopped and got out it had been totally quiet, like normal, but we had the music turned up loud in the car and it made things seem sort of hectic or like picturesque? With how far you could see across the fields, and the speed, and the light, and the music? Like when you're walking around with headphones on and it makes everything seem like a film? Like that. Anyway.

Josh was talking about setting up a business selling hand-made snacks. He said he wasn't going to go to university, he was going to make his fortune straight out of school. His big idea was that you could get these like gourmet snacks made to order, right there in the shop. It would be like the deli-counter of the munchie world, he was saying. He was laughing about it, but he was totally serious, he was laughing because he thought it was so brilliant. Any flavour you want, he was saying, any snack you want! I'll be a millionaire! He sounded like someone off *The Apprentice*. He was listing all the snacks he could think of, crisps and pretzels and Bombay mix and popcorn, and what they were all made of, and he was talking about how the economics of it were brilliant. Pennies into pounds, my friends! He kept shouting that. Pennies into pounds! He was shouting because the music was so loud but also because he was so excited about it? I didn't really get it. Anyway.

Tom wanted to know if this shop was going to be located round here and if so then where did Josh think his customer base was going to come from? It didn't look like Josh had thought about that. He waved his hand around a bit, meaning: like, around here somewhere? I don't know yet, he said. There's people around though, there's like a widely distributed customer base, yeah? He pointed to a farmhouse over on the right, three or four fields away, and then another one a bit further off, the other side of the river. The lights in the windows were just coming on so it must have been a bit darker by then than it seemed. There you go, he said, that's two of them right there. Tom said, what, are you going to do it like mobile? A mobile crisp van? Josh leaned over and punched him in the shoulder, and it was sort of a play-punch but he sort of meant it as well. No one said anything for a minute. It was just the music and the sound of the tyres on the road. I wasn't even sure where we were. I could see the red lights of some television mast or something, and the sky all shadowy blue behind it. We went over a little bridge and it felt like the tyres left the road for a second. I don't think Josh even knew where we were going. Josh said, don't take the piss mate. This is serious, this is totally serious. This is going to work, yeah? It's like, a totally unfulfilled market niche. And I'll be filling in that niche, big-time.

That got us laughing for a bit, about Josh filling in an unfulfilled niche.

Tom wouldn't let it go though, he was giving it all the economic model and the population density and the vulnerability of depending on impulse purchases and Josh was all nodding but then he goes Tom mate you don't get it. You don't get it. I'm talking about handmade gourmet snack products. Made to order! Like, locally sourced! They'll come pouring in from every direction! They'll be queuing up outside! He cut the music and put on this solemn face and a deep voice like from a film trailer and goes: If you fry it, they will come.

That set us off laughing again. The state we were in, it didn't take much? Plus Josh had this very high-pitched laugh that was pretty infectious, and once he'd got us all going it was just about impossible to stop? It just kept sort of growing, getting louder and louder, like something sort of swelling up until it filled the car and we couldn't hardly breathe and the noise of it was making me dizzy and then Amanda said Josh will you slow down a bit and he turned round to ask her what she'd said so that must have been how come he never saw the corner?

SUSWORTH

If It Keeps On Raining

Susworth

This is how his days begin. If you really want to know. Standing in his doorway in the cold, wet morning light and pissing on the stony ground. Waking up and getting out of bed and walking across the rough wooden floor. Opening the door and pulling down the front of his pyjamas and the weight of a whole night's piss pouring out on to the stony ground and winding down to the river which flows out to the sea. The relief of it. The long, sighing relief of it. He has to hold on to the doorframe to keep his balance.

He looks at the swirl and churn of the river. Boats passing, driftwood and debris. A drowned animal turning slowly in the current. Sometimes the people in the boats wave, but he doesn't wave back. He didn't ask them to come sweeping past like that while he's having his morning piss. In their shining white boats with the chrome guard-rails and the tinted windows and the little swim-decks on the stern. As if they'd ever swim in this river. They can come past if they like but they shouldn't expect him to wave. Not when his hands are full.

Sometimes there's a man fishing on the other side of the river. It's too far to see his face, so it's hard to tell whether the man can see what he's doing. But if he could he wouldn't be embarrassed. This is his house now, and there's nothing to stop him pissing on his own ground when he wakes up each day.

The boats mainly come past in the summer months, but the fisherman is there all year round. He brings a lot of accessories with him. He's got two or three different rods, and rests to set them in, and a big metal case that he sits on with all sorts of trays and drawers and compartments, and he keeps getting up to open all the drawers and trays. As if he's looking for something. As if he hasn't got any kind of an ordered storage system. He has this long net trailing in the water, with the open end pegged down on the bank. He uses it to keep the fish in once he's caught them. It's not clear why. Maybe he likes to count them. Or maybe he likes the way they look when he empties them back into the river, the silver flashes pouring through the air, the way they wriggle and flap for a second as though they were trying to fly. Or it could be for the company.

And he's got this other net, a big square net on the end of a long pole. If he gets fed up with all the rods and reels and maggots and not being able to find what he's looking for in those drawers, he could just sit on the edge of the bank and sweep it through the river until he comes up with something. Like a child at the seaside. Like a little boy with one of those coloured nets on the end of a bamboo cane.

Like a little boy whose dad was showing him how to use one of those nets, and lost it. At the seaside. When they were out on a jetty, and the boy's dad was sweeping the net back and forth through the clear salt-water, and the boy was pulling at his arm to say: Let me try let me have a go, and the man dropped it in the water somehow. The little boy wanted him to jump in and get it, and his father had to say: I'm sorry I can't. And the little boy wanted him to buy another one and the man had to say, again: I'm sorry I can't. The boy started crying and there wasn't much the man could do about it. He could have picked him up.

The way these things come into his head, sometimes. Standing there in the morning, looking at someone fishing, pissing on the stony ground that slopes down to the river, thinking about nothing much and then a man losing his little boy's net pops into his head from years back. This really was some years back now. The way he couldn't buy a new net to make it better. The little boy with his red hair.

He stands there each morning and he looks at the river, the fields, the sky. He tries to estimate what the weather will do for the rest of the day. He makes some decisions about the work he's going to do on the treehouse or the raft. He thinks about making breakfast. He thinks about going to look for more wood.

It's hard to understand why the people on the boats wave, sometimes. Perhaps they feel strange being out in the middle of the water like that. They feel vulnerable or lonely and it helps if they wave. Or they think it's just what they're supposed to do. Maybe they say ahoy! when they pass another boat. Who knows. The men on the commercial boats never wave. There's one that goes by about once a week, a gravel-barge, and he's never seen them waving the whole time he's been here, not at him or the man fishing or at any of the other boats. When it goes upstream it sits high on the water, its tall panelled sides beaten like a steel drum. But coming back down, fully loaded, it looks like a different boat, sunk low in the water, steady and slow, a man in a flat blue cap walking the wave-lapped gunwales and washing them down with a long-handled mop. And he wonders, often, what would happen if the man fell in, if he would prove to be a good swimmer, if the driver of the boat would be able to stop and pull him back on board. Or if the man would drown and wash on to the shore where this small piece of stony ground slopes down to the water.

He's not sure what he would do if that were to happen. If he would step down towards the man, and pick him up. Or at least drag him clear of the river. He's not sure if he'd be able to do it. Physically. Mentally. Maybe the right thing would be to wait for the proper authorities. Maybe his part could be to walk out along the road to the phone-box by the yacht club and do the necessary informing. They might come along and say: Thank you sir, you did the right thing. It was the right thing not to touch the body, well done. And take photos: of the stony ground, the body, the feet still paddling in the edge of the river. And people with the appropriate experience and accessories would come and pick him up, out of the water, and take him away.

They'd need the right accessories.

The other man on the boat wouldn't be able to help. It's a really big boat, he couldn't just steer it over to the bank and moor up and come running over shouting: Where is he, where is he, is he okay? It wouldn't be like that. He would have to continue his passage, steer the boat on to the nearest available pontoon and moor the boat securely, single-handed, and then come back to this location. And it's possible that by then the proper authorities would have been and gone, and taken his mop-dangling friend with them.

He imagines the skipper at the wheel of his heavy-laden barge, looking back at the spot in the river where his friend had slipped in. It would be difficult. Two men doing a job like that, every day, they could become very close. They could develop a close understanding of each other. Up and down the same stretch, loading and unloading, tying and untying, not saying much to each other because the noise of the engine would make it difficult to hear and because anyway what would there be to say. But understanding each other with a look and a nod, and a way of standing or a way of holding themselves, they could become very close, they would know each other better than perhaps they know anyone else. And then one of them slips from the wet gunwale into the water and his friend can only turn and look, the water closing over him as if nothing had happened and the long-handled mop floating down the river, out to sea.

He thinks about this a lot. But, who knows. It doesn't seem worth dwelling on. It seems an unlikely thing to need to consider, the proper procedure in such an event. But it's not an entirely unlikely occurrence. It happens. It has happened. People fall in the water, and they disappear, and they reappear drowned. It's not impossible. It's a thing that can happen.

Perhaps that's why the men on the barges don't wave. Because they're concentrating. They know about the things that can happen. They take the river seriously.

He watches them, when they pass, the man in the flat blue cap with the mop and the man at the wheel, and he wonders if they see him. If they see the man fishing, when he's there, which is quite often, or if they see anything besides the river and the current and the weather and each other.

He imagines they keep quite a close watch on the weather, the two of them. We've always got half an eye on it, they'd probably say, if someone asked them, if they came into the yacht club one evening and someone bought them a drink and talked to them about working that great boat up and down the river. It has quite an effect on our operation.

He keeps a close watch on the weather as well, from his place on the riverbank. It changes quite slowly. He can see it happening in the distance: a break in the clouds, a veil of rain rolling in across the fields. Sometimes he thinks it would be interesting to keep a chart of it. Windspeeds, temperatures, total rainfall, that type of thing. But it would need certain equipment, certain know-how and measuring equipment, and he's not sure where someone would come by that type of thing. Probably it would mean going into town.

But sometimes it can really take his breath away, how different this place can look, with a change in the weather. He can stand in the doorway, first thing in the morning, and all the rain from the day before has vanished and there are no clouds and it looks like maybe there never were any clouds and there never will be again, the sky is that clear and clean and huge, and everything that was grey before is fresh and bright like newly sawn wood. And then other times he can stand here and see nothing, the thick mist lifting up off the river and nothing visible besides the trees around his house. The river just a muffled sound of water rushing over the stony banks. The opposite bank completely lost, and no clue as to whether the fisherman is there or not with his rods and his accessories. The fisherman doesn't seem the sort to let a damp day put him off his fishing, but there's no way of knowing.

It's frustrating, not being able to know. He's a man who likes to know these things. What's happening in his immediate surroundings. The lie of the land. Sometimes he's even thought about walking round to the man's spot to find out, to make sure. But it's a long walk, and there are things he has to do with his time. It would be about six miles altogether, out along the road past the yacht club, into the village, past the post office, out by the farm to the new road bridge and then all the way back along the other bank.

And what would he say to him when he got there anyway. It would be awkward.

People call it the new road bridge, but it must be twenty or thirty years old.

It's not just the weather that changes. It's surprising, how new a day can look, how different the view can be when he stands there each morning having a piss on the stony ground. The height of the water, the colour of the sky, the feel of the air against his skin, the direction of the smoke drifting out from the cooling towers along the horizon, the number of leaves on the trees, the footprints of birds and small animals in the soft mud at the water's edge, the colour of the river running by.

The speed of the water changes, that's something else, with the height of the river. If it's been raining a lot. The river draws itself up, the water churning brown with all the mud washed in off the fields, and the river rises up and races towards the sea, sweeping round bends and rushing over rocks or trees or sunken boats that sit and rest in its way, anything that thinks it can just rest where it is, the river rushes over and picks it up and carries it along, like loose soil and stones on the banks of outside bends, or trees with fragile roots, or a stack of pallets left too close to the water's edge, it all gets swept along, like people in a crowd, like what happens in a football ground if there are too many people in not enough space and something happens to make everyone rush, if they all start to run and then no one person can stop or avoid it, they all move together and then what can anyone expect if there's a dam been put up against all that momentum, if there's a fence and someone saying stand back don't run there's enough room for everyone if you could spread out and stand back and just stop pushing.

When there's not enough room. When there's too many of them and someone puts up a fence and says stop pushing.

That's what it's like. The river. When it's been raining too much. The momentum of it is huge and dangerous: it makes him think of a crowd of people being swept along and none of them can stop it and they get to a fence and someone says stop pushing. In a football ground. Everybody rushing into one space and there's not enough room and no one can stop moving. And there's a fence and someone standing behind the fence says: Stop pushing will you all please stop pushing.

65

It's what comes to mind, when he sees the river like that.

And other times the river is quiet. After the rain has stopped. After a few days of the river raging past, all choked with mud and fury, it drops back down again; slows, slips away from the high carved banks and comes to what looks like a standstill. The sun in broken shards across its surface, like scraps of tinfoil thrown from a bridge by some children further upstream. It looks good enough to swim in, then. Not that he ever has. He's never seen anyone swimming here. It doesn't seem like a good idea.

*

So. This is how his days begin. If you really want to know. The morning creeps through the cracked windows of his house. He stands in the doorway, pissing on the stony ground, and he thinks about all these things. He looks at the river, and the sky, and the weather, and he thinks about his work for the day. He tries to allocate his priorities. The treehouse is almost finished, apart from the roof, but the raft is still a long way from being done.

The roof will be important.

He thinks about the people on the boats, and the man fishing, and children further upstream throwing things into the water. Throwing sticks and model boats, pieces of paper jammed into plastic bottles with screw-top lids. He imagines the bottles washing up on to his piece of land by chance, and he imagines unscrewing the lids and unrolling the pieces of paper. He thinks about the children, on the bridge, watching the model boats and the plastic bottles turning in the current. He imagines them shielding their eyes to catch a last glimpse. Two of them, a boy and a girl, the girl almost eleven now, the boy eight and a half. Red-haired, like their father. He imagines the girl turning away and saying: Come on, we should catch up with Mum now, and the boy saying: But I can still see mine, I can. Holding his small hands up to his eyes like binoculars.

And what would be written, on these pieces of paper?

The sky looks clear right across to the far field, a faint early sun shining off the river. But there's a cold wind, and rain on the way.

Yellowed willow leaves blow across the stony ground and into the river, floating away like tiny boats heading out to sea.

And when it starts they won't understand. They'll put on coats and go outside, brandishing umbrellas against the violence of the sky. They'll check the forecast and wait for the rain to stop so they can hang the washing outside. But it won't stop. They should understand, but they won't.

The treehouse is almost done. It was slow when he started; he didn't really know what he was doing. He had to try a few different techniques before he could progress. There was less urgency then. There's more now. It's sort of imperative that he gets it finished soon. He's used pallets mostly. They're easy to get hold of, and if it looks a bit untidy then so what. At least it does the job.

Some of the others in the yacht club have noticed. They must have seen it from the road when they were driving past. They were laughing about it last time he went in. One of them asked if his name was Robinson and where was the rest of the Swiss family, and he almost did something then, like swinging a big glass ashtray into the side of his head or pushing him off his stool. But he didn't. He's more careful now. Accidents and things like that happen very easily, if he's not careful. So he didn't say a thing. They asked him lots of questions, like what was he building it for and why was it so high and what was he going to do when the winds picked up. He just said he had some wood lying around and he thought he'd give it a go, and when someone beat their chest and made a noise like Tarzan he got up and left. He didn't even slam the door, and he didn't go back when he heard them laugh.

Who knows why they call it the yacht club. None of them have got yachts.

The way they laughed. Some people deserve it, what will come.

It might not be the finest treehouse ever built, but it does what it needs to do. It's difficult to get the details exactly right when you're fifty foot up in the air. It's hard enough getting all the wood up there in the first place. It would be easier with two people. Or quicker, at least. But it's just him, now, so it takes some careful planning. Some forethought. And hard work.

He needs some roofing felt. Or an old tarpaulin, if he can't find any felt. The roof will be important. He'll need to take his time over the roof. And then there's the raft, of course: he's got the basic structure, the barrels and the pallets, but it needs more work on the lashings. It's the structural integrity which will count, in the long run. It might need some kind of shelter as well, a little cabin or a frame for a tarpaulin. If it can take the weight.

The weather, when it changes, generally comes rolling in from the east. He can stand here and watch the clouds gathering, like an army forming up in the distance and preparing to march. Only when it comes in it's more of a charge than a march, crashing into the river, with a noise like boxes of nails spilling on to a wooden floor. When it comes like that, furious and sudden, it usually passes by again soon enough, the air beaten clean in its wake.

But there will come a time when it doesn't pass. When the clouds gather and don't pass away, and rain pours endlessly upon the earth. And some will be prepared, and some will not.

He wonders what the man on the other side of the river does, when he's not here. When he's not fishing. Probably he's retired and that's why he can manage to be here so often. But he doesn't look old enough to be retired, the way he walks, the weight he carries. Maybe he got grounds of ill health out of someone, out of whoever he was working for. The police, maybe, it's quite possible to get grounds of ill health with the police, like mental distress for example, like if something were to happen, there are things that can happen if you work in the police, there are things that can give you stress or mental distress. For example things you might witness or be a part of.

Like being in front of a crowd, and saying: Stop pushing there's enough room for everyone there's no need to push. Like being the other side of a fence and saying: Get back stop pushing. And then later you see the rails, steel rails, bent and broken as easily as reeds.

It could be difficult for someone to do their job after something like that, to carry that with them and not be affected by the mental distress. Fishing might be an ideal respite: the order of it, the quietness, the solitude. No one shouting or pushing. No one asking for explanations. Just the river, easing on past. The sky, the changing light, the flash of silver from the emptying net when the fish pour safely back into the river.

It might not be that, of course. That would just be speculation. It might be nothing like that at all.

When it comes it will come suddenly, rushing across the earth like a vengeful crowd, an unturnable tide of seething fury. They will stand and watch, in bus shelters, in shop doorways, from the apparent safety of locked cars, and they will tut to themselves and say: Oh, isn't the weather awful, and they will not know what they say.

And those two children on the bridge, throwing scraps of paper into the water, watching the water rise higher, perhaps they will have the sense to know what is happening, perhaps they will climb a tree and scan the horizon for a place of safety. Or perhaps in desperation they will take their umbrellas and turn them into boats, drop them into the river and ride them wherever the current goes. Or perhaps they're too big for that now.

And whenever it looks as though the rain will stop, people will come out of their houses and peer up at the sky. They will lift their faces and let themselves be soaked while they stare at the thinning clouds, retreating to the safety of their houses, their upstairs bedrooms, their rooftops.

This will be in the first few weeks. Before they realise.

When it happens there will be people rushing by, the torrential current of the new river sweeping them quickly and terribly past. And he won't be able to help them. But he'll look, and if he sees two little ones hurtling along, two red-haired, wide-eyed little ones, he'll reach out with a big net on the end of a long pole he's got there ready, and he'll pull them in, dry them off and wrap them up warm and cook them supper. And they can all stay together in

71

the treehouse for as long as it takes, and if the children get bored there will be paper and crayons for them to draw with, write messages on, make little model boats from. And if they need to leave they'll have the raft. They'll be ready.

The sky is clear now, but the rain is coming. He can smell it.

Sometimes when he wakes it's still only just getting light. It's good, to stand there and watch the morning creep up on the world, the river a shadow in front of him, the cold air against his skin. It's a privilege. Sometimes he can just stand there for a whole hour, watching the shapes and colours taking form out of the darkness. The streams and ditches all glinting like silver threads.

It is sometimes a very beautiful world. It's a shame, what will happen.

It's rare, though, to spend an hour watching the morning arrive like that. People don't. It's rare for people to even spend a moment enjoying their first piss of the day, the way he does. People are so busy. They'll brush their teeth sitting on the toilet to save a few minutes. Eat breakfast standing up. They don't have the time to watch the colour bleed into the world each day. They have meetings, schedules, documents. They don't have time to listen to each other, to be patient with the difficulties of expression. They haven't got the time to stand and watch a man say nothing except: I can't explain, or: I don't know how to say it. There are important things to be done, and a man who will spend a day standing at a window is not a man who can fit into such functional and fulfilling lives.

These are not people with ears to hear or eyes to see. These are not people who will understand, when it comes.

They will say they understand. They will say they know it might take a while to come to terms. But one day there will be shouting, there will be a cracked voice saying: I don't have time to deal with all this. There will be the banging of objects against hard surfaces, a waving of arms, children standing and crying.

They don't have time. They have busy and important things to do. They need somebody who can be there for them. They need somebody who can go back to work, even after that. Silence and stillness and contemplation aren't going to pay the bills.

This is how his days begin, now. He asked me to tell you. He wakes up, he walks across the rough wooden floor, he holds on to the doorframe and he pisses on to the stony ground.

He looks at the height of the river and the colour of the sky. He looks up at the half-built treehouse, and the raft, and he plans his work for the day.

Soon it will rain. And people won't understand. They'll just put on their hats and coats, open their umbrellas, and rush out into the middle of whatever it is they need to do. Their busy days. Their successful and important lives.

He thought you should know.

Fleeing Complexity

Irby in the Marsh

The fire spread quicker than the little bastard was expecting.

Vessel

Halton Holegate

She took the tulips from his hands. Let me find something to put those in, she said. His hands were cold. She
was surprised that he'd come and she wanted to cover her
surprise. She laid the tulips on the kitchen counter and
looked around for a pair of scissors. The flower-heads
were still tightly closed. The petals were red, with a rim
of yellow at the lips. The stems arched, the way that tulip
stems always did. She would need a vase tall enough to
bear their weight. She picked them up and put them down.
She didn't know where the scissors were. She opened a
drawer. She stopped; she'd forgotten to invite him in. He
must still be standing on the doorstep, in the snow. She
felt the cold air blowing through from the hallway. By the
time she got back to him he'd stepped forward as far as the
runner and was standing with the door half-closed behind
him. Oh come in, of course, come in, she said. You weren't
waiting to be asked were you? He smiled, and shrugged,

and snow fell from his shoulders as he crooked up a leg to wrestle off a shoe. She watched. She wanted to brush the snow from him and take his coat, put a hand against his cold cheek. She waited.

She lit the burner and put the kettle on. She wondered what he was doing here. They had a conversation, of sorts, standing there in the kitchen.

'You didn't walk, in this weather?'

'I got the bus. I walked from the end of the village. Where the bus turns.'

'I'm surprised the bus was running.'

'I wasn't sure it would.'

'And you didn't think of calling first, to check I'd be here?'

'I felt like taking a chance. I had the afternoon free.'

'Well. It is nice to see you. It's a nice surprise. Tea?'

'Please. Milk, if you have any.'

She poured the boiling water into a pot and the milk into a jug. She put them on a tray with cups and saucers and the sugar bowl. She carried the tray through to the front room and they sat across from each other while the snow fell past the bright window and the tea steeped and swirled inside the pot.

'These are nice cups.'

'Aren't they? We've had them a long time. They were a wedding present.'

'Really? I don't remember seeing them before.'

'Well, no. James never really liked them.'

'Ah.'

'So they were put away.'

'Yes.'

'But now, I thought, I mean. You know.'

'Are they French?'

'Flemish, I think.'

'They're very nice.'

'Yes.'

'They sit well in your hand, don't they? They have a nice weight.'

'Yes. I suppose they do.'

'I'm sorry. About James.'

'Yes.'

'You got my card?'

'Oh. I don't think so. No.'

'Oh, I'm sorry. The post hasn't been what it was, has it?'

'No, it really hasn't. Excuse me.'

She'd forgotten to put the tulips in something. She hadn't even got as far as cutting the stems. She wondered why he'd come today; what was different about today. She opened a drawer. She found the scissors on the side, by the draining board. She cut the twine and the tulips rolled out across the worktop. She looked for the little sachet of plant-food, but of course there wasn't one. It was just like him, not to have said he was coming. James would never have done such a thing. But neither would James have thought to bring flowers. She cut the ends off the tulip stems, scooping them up and dropping them in the compost-bin. She remembered where the vases were, and that she couldn't reach them. She didn't want to clamber up on a stool to fetch one down. She asked him if he minded and he said not at all. Of course, he

78

could reach the top cupboard without even stretching up on his toes. James would have needed to stretch, at least. It was a nice vase he chose. It was the right one: tall enough to support the arching stems, narrow enough to hold them closely, subtle enough not to detract from their colour.

'Wherever did you find flowers, anyway?'

'Oh, you know. You can still find these things, if you look.'

'It's a long time since I've seen cut flowers.'

'You just have to know the right people, that's all.'

'And you do.'

'I manage. You're still getting milk?'

'Straight from the farm.'

'There hasn't been any in town for a time.'

'You don't know the right people for milk, then?'

'I didn't. But I've got you now, haven't I?'

She didn't know about that. She didn't know about that at all. It seemed somehow presumptuous. He must know there was a limited supply. She didn't say anything, and he seemed to realise that he'd overstepped the mark because he moved towards the window and started talking about the garden, about how difficult it was to start things off with the snows getting later and later like this. She looked at the back of him while he spoke. How very upright he was, even at his age. He'd always been one of the standing-up-straight sort. Proper. It was certainly nice to see him again. But she didn't know what he thought he was doing here. She carried the vase of tulips into the front room and set them on the coffee table, where they would best hold the light. He followed her through, slightly unexpectedly,

79

and, standing a little too close, asked whether she'd ever considered taking in paying guests. She told him she didn't really know about that.

'You have the space though.'

'Well, perhaps.'

'I just rather wondered whether you couldn't use the extra hands about the place. You know. I realise money's not quite the thing at the moment, but there could be other forms of payment. Help, you know. Connections.'

'I'm not sure, really.'

'I do have a strong back, even now. There's lots I could do.'

'I have people who come and help, thank you. I manage.'

'It's just that, you know how it is. Things are rather difficult. In town. I thought we might be able to help each other out. At a difficult moment. For old times' sake. A mutually beneficial arrangement, you know.'

'I don't think it's very practical, actually.'

'It's completely practical!'

'Excuse me.'

'Oh, now.'

'I think the bus may be leaving soon.'

'Look, sorry.'

'I wouldn't want you to miss it.'

'Will you think about it though? Will you be in touch?'

'I think you'd better get on. If you're to catch that bus.'

'Mary, will you think about it?'

'Thank you very much for the flowers. They really are lovely. I do appreciate the trouble you must have gone to in finding them.'

'Mary, please.'

She moved into the hallway and held out his coat, waiting for him to put his shoes back on. She held it out between them, as though to forestall him. She couldn't bear a scene. He opened the door and took his coat and ducked his head beneath the falling snow. He didn't look at her as he left. She closed the door to keep the heat in. She watched him through the spyhole. The lens made him appear warped, smaller than he really was.

Which Reminded Her, Later

Grantham

And then there was the American woman he'd offered the spare room to that time, without question or thought or apparent consideration of the fact that Catherine might at least like to have been told. The first she'd known about it had been when she'd got home from work and found the woman standing there in the hallway, looking not at all surprised or uncomfortable, eating natural yoghurt straight from the pot and waiting for whatever it was that Catherine was going to say. Which had of course been nothing more than a faintly quizzical *hello?* Holding the front door open behind her, the rain blowing in from the garden and something like smugness or amusement lingering on the American woman's face for just a moment before she finally acknowledged Catherine with a quietly unconcerned *hello* of her own. And carried on eating the yoghurt. And made no attempt to explain herself.

A strange-looking woman, she remembered. Very slim, and very pale, with rubbed-red eyes and mismatched layers of clothing; a long cotton dress, a man's checked shirt, a college scarf, a beige raincoat. Sandals. No make-up. She looked at first as though she might be in her sixties, but Michael said later that he'd thought she was closer to forty-five. Which was their own age at the time, in fact.

'Can I help you?' Catherine had asked, only slightly more pointedly – strange, this reluctance to be more direct, to say who the hell are you and do you mind getting out of my house – and the woman had shaken her head, and smiled graciously, and said, 'Oh, no, thank you, your husband's been very kind already.' Holding up the yoghurt spoon to demonstrate what kindness she'd been shown. At which point Michael had appeared, loitering purposefully in the study doorway, and Catherine had understood the situation, had gone straight through to the kitchen without another word to take off her wet coat and sit at the table and wait for something like an explanation while the woman drifted away upstairs.

The woman had been in a bit of a situation, apparently. That was what she'd told Michael, and that was what he told Catherine when he followed her through to the kitchen and sat at the table to explain. She wasn't someone who went about asking like this, she'd told him, but she wasn't sure what else she could do. She'd come over for some medical treatment, she'd heard that the hospital here was a world-renowned centre for people with her condition, and of course she hadn't thought she'd need worry about accommodation, it being a hospital and everything, only now there'd been some difficulty about being admitted, a difficulty she was never very clear about but which seemed to involve documents she didn't have, and she should have foreseen that, of course, she knew she should, but people with her condition tended to grab at possibilities and this is a world-renowned centre we're talking about at the hospital here and logistics came second to hope sometimes, Michael understood that, didn't he? But the thing was she'd spent all her money getting here and so just for now she was in this sort of, well, this situation. If he knew what she was saying.

That first conversation had taken place at the church. People often went there looking for help, and Michael almost always gave them something: food, or money, or the address of somewhere else they could go. Sometimes it was enough that he didn't just shut the door in their faces, that he listened to their long explanations of funerals to be attended, school trips to be paid for, faulty gas meters and lost cheques and misunderstandings over benefit forms. He wasn't naive; he knew when to say no. It was just that he didn't always think being spun a yarn was a good enough reason for not doing what he could to help. *It's the desperate ones who come up with the best stories*, he used to say, and Catherine had admired him for this, once, for his refusal to let cynicism accumulate with each knock at the church office door. She wasn't capable of such a refusal, she knew. She'd grown cynical in her own job a long time ago, listening to students mumble excuses about late and inadequate coursework, attending departmental meetings where people used phrases like *rebranding the undergraduate experience*. And then coming home from one of those meetings to find a strange American woman eating yoghurt in her hallway.

They'd had people staying before, of course. That wasn't new. Lodgers, friends of friends, people like this woman who just turned up at the church needing somewhere to stay. Catherine didn't usually mind. Vicarages were big houses, and they had plenty of spare rooms. Michael seemed to consider it as much a part of his job as the visiting, the preaching, the offering of communion; or not even as part of his job so much as part of his life. *What does our faith mean, if we don't do these things for even the least among us?* She'd heard him say that in his sermons, many times, and she'd been thrilled by how sincerely he'd seemed to mean it, once.

She'd asked him how long the American woman was going to stay and he'd said not long. A couple of nights, three at most. Maybe four. She'd asked him why he hadn't talked to her first, and he'd said he hadn't really had the chance and didn't she trust his judgment? She'd asked what sort of condition the woman had that would bring her all this way to find treatment, and he'd said that he wasn't sure, that the woman hadn't been specific but that he'd got the impression it was some kind of bone disease. Something quite rare, he'd said, and she'd raised her eyebrows, and made a disbelieving face, and said that he wasn't making any sense, the story didn't make any sense. Which he'd pretended to ignore, and so when they'd made dinner then it had been in a bristling near-silence. Catherine boiling and draining and mashing the potatoes, adding butter and milk and salt. Michael turning the sausages under the grill, setting the table, stirring the gravy, disappearing upstairs to ask the woman to join them, coming back to report that she'd said she wasn't hungry and she didn't want to put them out. Moving around each other with a practised ease, passing forks and spoons and stock cubes from hand to hand without needing to be asked, and by the time they were sitting at the table and giving thanks her irritation had faded enough for her to be able to check what the woman's name was. Michael said he didn't know. He hadn't asked, or she hadn't said, and the whole time she was there they only ever referred to her as this woman or the American woman or most of the time just a shorthanded her or she. When are you going to talk to *her*. What's *she* doing here. How much longer is *she* going to stay.

The whole business should have been the final straw, Catherine thought.

The day after she arrived, the American woman went back to the hospital – they knew this because she left a note in the hallway which said GONE TO HOSPITAL in thick capital letters – and when she came back, early in the afternoon, she went straight up to the spare room without telling Michael what the result of her visit had been. The same thing happened, complete with a second note – GONE TO HOSPITAL, AGAIN – the day after that. On Sunday the woman stayed in her room all day, and when Catherine knocked on her door around suppertime she was met with a sudden taut silence, as if the woman had been pacing around and had now stopped, her breath held, listening. Catherine knocked again.

'Who is it?' the woman said. 'Who's there?' This said suspiciously, almost aggressively. Catherine hesitated.

'It's Catherine,' she said. She half thought, since they hadn't been properly introduced, that she should add something like *Michael's wife*, or possibly even *the vicar's wife*, for clarification. But she didn't. The American woman jerked the door open and stepped forwards, standing a little closer than Catherine would have liked, wearing the same mismatch of clothes she'd been wearing when she arrived. She didn't say anything. She seemed to be waiting for Catherine to speak. It was infuriating, this misplaced sense of – what was it, self-assurance? Self-possession?

'We were just wondering if everything was okay,' Catherine said. Speaking calmly, she hoped. 'We were wondering if you needed anything,' she added. The woman seemed to relax slightly.

'I'm fine,' she said. 'Thank you for asking.'

'Have you had any luck at the hospital?' Catherine asked. 'With your documents and everything?' The woman smiled.

'Oh, you know what these places are like,' she said, waving her hand dismissively; 'it's all forms to fill out and papers to sign and documents to produce, it's all just bureaucracy, isn't it?'

Catherine looked at the woman, and noticed again how thin and pale she was. A little powder would have helped, a spot of colour, something around the eyes. She looked so drained. But she was probably the sort of woman who would disapprove of make-up.

'Do you mind if I ask what your condition is exactly?' Catherine said, speaking more abruptly than she'd intended. The woman looked at her a moment, blinking fiercely, as if she had something in her eye.

'I'll be going back there in the morning,' she said, ignoring the question. 'Maybe I can resolve the matter then and be out of your way.'

'Oh?' said Catherine. 'Do you know how long you'll be? Because Michael and I will both be out until quite late.' The woman smiled, and started to close the door.

'Oh, no,' she said, 'it's okay. I can let myself in, thank you.'

Catherine found Michael downstairs, sleeping in the armchair, and asked him if he'd given the woman a key. He stirred slightly, and sections of the weekend paper slipped from his lap to the floor. Catherine repeated the question, and he opened one eye to look at her. 'It seemed like a good idea at the time,' he said.

Which had reminded her, later, of the morning after the first night they'd spent together, and of him lying in bed with one eye open just like that, watching her dress. Because he'd thought he was dreaming and didn't want to wake up, he'd said. It hadn't looked like that, she'd told him, buttoning her blouse and looking around the room for her stockings; it had looked more like he was spying on her. She'd loved him watching her like that, then. *And you a man of the cloth as well.* This said when the idea of him as a vicar was some kind of joke still, before he was ordained; before they were married even, although there'd been some prevarication around that *before*, around whether they hadn't better wait, which they'd settled by deciding that engagement was a commitment in itself and they were as good as married in God's eyes. She remembered their haste over dinner that night, once the decision had been made; barely tasting the food, barely even speaking, catching a bus back to his friend's flat while most people were only just heading out for the night. And then the heat and hurry of first sex, collapsing all too soon under the weight of expectation. The realisation that this, after all, was something else which would have to be learnt, considered, practised.

And what were they then, twenty-one, twenty-two? More than half a life ago now. Graduates, just, and already moving on to the next thing. Michael at theological college, preparing for ministry, talking about curacies and parishes and the discernment of vocation; Catherine less certain, knowing only that she wanted to carry on studying English, that she didn't want to fall into teaching the way so many of her friends had done. No more than two years since they'd met, volunteering at the chaplaincy's soup run – Michael overflowing with the thrill of new belief, Catherine looking for some way to rekindle a childhood faith which had been more inheritance than choice – and already the thought of them not being together had seemed puzzling and unreal. As if they had been brought inevitably to one another. Which she'd believed, then. Their life together had been so filled with purpose that it had felt like something more than chance: the soup-run project, and the Christmas night shelter they'd helped set up; the prayer vigils they'd organised, the 24-hour fasts; and that summer in Europe, sleeping in train stations and parks, going to free concerts in bombed-out churches, sharing open-air communion with Germans and Italians and Norwegians and thinking that this was how life would be for them now, that this endless sense of possibility was what her faith could finally come to mean.

And then there was marriage, ordination, a first curacy, a flat. A master's degree, a PhD proposal, a funding problem, and falling into teaching term by term. All these things decided, settled, while they were still too young to know any better. You can go back to the research later though, Michael had told her, when the PhD fell through and she found herself accepting teaching work after all; there wasn't any rush. Trying to reassure her. Keeping one eye on what she was doing.

On Monday morning they found the yoghurt spoon outside the American woman's room, with a note. THANK YOU FOR THE SPOON, it said. Catherine knocked at the door, and waited a moment before peering inside. The bed was made, and the holdall the woman had brought with her was gone. But there were still clothes in the wardrobe, and a scarf hanging on the back of the door.

'She hasn't left then,' Catherine said.

'Doesn't look like it,' Michael said, already turning away.

'She might have just forgotten to pack everything.'

'Maybe,' he said, in a tone which suggested it was unlikely, and went downstairs. She closed the door and followed him, picking up the post and dropping it on the kitchen table while Michael put the kettle on to boil. She cut two slices of bread and put them in the toaster, and Michael fetched plates and knives and butter and honey from the cupboard. Unthinking, this routine. Unbreakable, almost.

'I don't like her,' Catherine announced. Michael looked at her strangely.

'Like her?' he said. 'You don't even know her. Why would you like her or not like her?' The toaster popped up before the toast was ready, as it always did. Something was wrong with the timer, apparently. Nothing which couldn't be fixed. Catherine reached over and put it down again.

'There's something about her,' she said. 'She makes me uncomfortable. The way she looks at me. The way she seems to be taking us for granted.' Michael filled the teapot, put it on the table, and sat down.

'The way she looks at you?' he repeated. He seemed amused. The toaster popped up, and she put it down again.

'And the way she won't answer my questions,' she added. Michael made a noise in the back of his throat, something like a snort or a stopped chuckle. A harrumph, people would once have called it. She'd married a man who harrumphed at her across the breakfast table. The toaster popped up a third time. She brought the toast to the table and passed it over to him. 'What's she doing here, Michael?' she asked, sharply. 'What's she doing in our house? She could be anyone. We don't even know her name.' He finished buttering his toast before replying, and she saw, in his expression, that same infuriating self-assurance which the American woman had shown her.

'First,' he said, 'it's not our house. It's a vicarage. It belongs to the church, and we're guests here just as much as she is.' Catherine tried to cut in, but he held up a finger to stop her. Actually held up a finger. When had he started doing this? Why had she never said anything?

'Second,' he continued, 'this woman came to me asking for help, and regardless of whether she's odd or evasive or whether she's even telling the truth I don't see that any harm can come of offering her a room for a few nights. It's not as if we need it.' He poured the tea, sliding hers across the table and reaching for the pile of post. 'But if you think I've made a mistake,' he said, 'you're welcome to ask her to leave.'

There was a word for this, for the way he was being about this whole thing – superior? Supercilious? And there was a word for women like her who put up with this kind of behaviour for as long as she had – a word like, what, weak? Not weak exactly, it was more complicated than that, but not decisive, not assertive. Not when it mattered. She stood up, leaving the tea on the table and her toast uneaten. She'd given up slamming doors a long time ago, so instead she just left it gaping open and went upstairs to get ready for work.

Work was a lecturing post in the English department at the new university. She hadn't ever got back to the research. There weren't all that many research positions available in the English departments of new universities. She wrote the odd paper here and there, did her bit to keep the research assessment scores at a respectable level, but mostly she concentrated on shepherding her students through the set texts and critical literature; giving lectures and seminars, setting essays and marking essays and trying to keep up with all the paperwork which had lately crept into the job.

It was a good job though. She liked it. She couldn't remember, now, why she had once been so determined to avoid teaching. She enjoyed standing in front of a group of students and helping them work their way towards an understanding of what literature could do, what it did do. *Developing the analytical tools*, it was called these days, although she preferred her first departmental head's description of it as *turning the lights on in there*.

She liked being in an environment where people enjoyed what they were doing, valued it, even if they tried to pretend they didn't. She liked having colleagues at all – she'd seen how Michael's solitary, self-directed work had isolated him at times, turned him in on himself – and she enjoyed just sitting in the staffroom with them, drinking coffee, talking, listening to gossip. Of which there seemed only to be more the older they got; some of her colleagues were divorced already, one more than once, and over the years there'd been regular talk of goings on behind marital backs. She'd even, once, found herself in a situation where it had been made clear that something like that had been an option for her. But the idea had seemed absurd, a caricature of any discontent she might have been feeling, and she'd declined. She wondered if that had ever been gossiped about around the coffee table there, with the curled-corner posters of fat new novels stuck to the walls and the ring-binders stacked in the corner behind the door. It seemed unlikely.

When she got home that afternoon, Michael showed her a note he'd found on the desk in his study. WOULD APPRECIATE FEWER QUESTIONS, it said; MY CONDITION DOES NOT RESPOND WELL TO STRESS.

'You have to ask her to leave,' Catherine said. Michael made a non-committal sound, an *mm* or an *umm*, and Catherine waited for something more.

'It's quite a statement though, isn't it?' he said. 'What did you say to the woman?'

'Michael, please. I'm just not comfortable with her being in the house,' Catherine said.

'Do you think she's on some kind of fast?' Michael asked. Catherine took the note from his hand and looked at it again. 'What?' she said.

'Do you think she's fasting?' he repeated.

'I don't know, Michael,' she said, 'I really don't know.' She was suddenly very tired.

'Because as far as I can see she's only eating yoghurt,' he said. 'Have you noticed her eating anything else? She hasn't asked to use the kitchen. She's never joined us for dinner, she keeps insisting on not being hungry. Haven't you noticed?' He seemed fascinated by the idea.

'Michael,' Catherine said. He looked up. 'She can't stay.'

The woman came back late. They heard her letting herself in while they were clearing away the dinner things, and by the time Catherine had got out to the hallway she was halfway up the stairs.

'Hello again,' Catherine said. The woman turned round, the holdall in one hand and a carrier bag filled with pots of yoghurt in the other.

'Hey,' she said. Her hair was hanging limply around her face, and her skin was even paler than it had been before. She looked exhausted, ill.

'No luck at the hospital?' Catherine asked. The woman stared at her.

'Does it look like it?' she said, turning away. She was almost at the top of the stairs before Catherine could take a breath and respond.

'Excuse me,' she said, raising her voice a little. 'Sorry?' The woman stopped, but didn't turn round. 'Sorry,' Catherine said again, trying to soften her voice with a laugh; 'but I was just wondering. I mean, we don't actually know each other's names, do we?' Waiting for the woman to turn round, feeling her fists almost clenching when she didn't. 'My name's Catherine,' she called up.

'Hello, Catherine,' the woman said, flatly, and continued on up the stairs to her room.

Catherine stood in the hallway, waiting for something, unwilling to go straight back to the kitchen and have Michael ask about her day and what they might watch on the television as if nothing untoward was going on. As if the woman wasn't staying longer than he'd said she would. As if the woman had been open and straightforward with them and given them no cause for concern.

She prayed about it later that evening, sitting in the front room with a lit candle and a Bible on the coffee table, a confused prayer in which she asked that they all be kept safe, that her fears about the woman prove unfounded, that the woman find what she was looking for at the hospital, that Michael or herself might find some way of resolving the situation, that she could be less suspicious and more trusting of the world and the people who came her way, that God might grant her more love and faith and empathy in situations like this, that Michael might listen to her a little more, take her fears more seriously, that God might watch over them all in this situation.

She opened her eyes, and saw the woman standing in the doorway, still wearing the long beige raincoat and holding another spoon. Smiling.

'I'm sorry,' the woman said. 'I didn't mean to intrude. I just thought I heard something.'

'Well,' Catherine said. 'Only me.' She felt as if she'd been caught out, exposed somehow. The woman smiled, and that self-assurance, self-contentment, self-whatever-it-was, was there again.

'Yes,' she said. 'Only you.' She noticed Catherine looking at the spoon. 'Oh,' she said, 'I hope you don't mind. I helped myself to a spoon, for the yoghurt.' Pronouncing yoghurt with a long *oh*, which in Catherine's irritable state felt like yet another trespass.

'Oh no,' Catherine replied, lifting her hands in an attempt at nonchalance, letting them clap down on her thighs; 'that's fine. It's only a spoon.' A weak smile, met with a shrug. The woman glanced down at the Bible, the candle.

'Were you praying?' she asked. Catherine nodded, and the woman looked puzzled, tilting her head as if she was about to ask something. 'Well,' she said, finally, 'I won't keep you. It sounds like your husband's gone to bed already.'

'Goodnight,' Catherine said. The woman left, closing the door behind her, and Catherine watched as the candle flame flapped and fluttered and eventually stilled.

* * *

96

She shouldn't be angry though. It wasn't fair. She shouldn't have been angry at the time, and she should have learnt not to be still angry about these things now. He was dedicated to his job. He cared about the church, about the redevelopment, about the new community services he wanted to offer, about enthusing the congregation with a sense of mission. These were all good things to care about, to spend every waking moment worrying about. But she was tired of it now. She was tired of being towed along while he did these things.

At least people didn't come calling to the house, generally. That was one thing. It happened to other vicars – it had happened in previous parishes – but it hadn't happened here. The vicarage was too far from the church, too anonymous-looking, and so they hadn't had people banging on the door at all hours asking for money as they had elsewhere. People went to the church, and Michael dealt with them there. Which was good. It gave them some separation, mostly. It meant Michael could relax a little once he was home, and it meant Catherine had to worry a little less about always being The Vicar's Wife. There were still the phone calls of course, and the members of the congregation who knew where they lived and would insist on calling round with messages, paperwork, problems, and would talk to her when Michael was out as if she was his secretary. She'd minded it more in the early days, before she'd felt established in her career. She'd resented the idea that her role in the world might amount to no more than being The Vicar's Wife. I married you, she'd snapped at him once; I didn't marry your job. I didn't marry the Church.

That had been their first crisis. There had been others: his muted, slow-burning reaction to his mother's death, when he'd shut her out so completely that she'd almost walked away; the string of burglaries in the last parish; the incident which never was with her colleague in the English department. And there was the business of children, of course, but they'd stopped talking about that eventually, once it had become more or less academic.

And then there was the American woman he'd offered the spare room to that time, six years ago now and she couldn't help thinking it was too long ago for her to be still thinking about it like this. It wasn't as if they'd ever seen her again.

That Saturday, when the woman had been in their house for more than a week and was showing no sign of being about to leave, Catherine had been woken by the sound of Michael making his breakfast. She usually tried to have a lie-in on Saturdays, and was usually woken like this, by the clatter of knives and plates and mugs, reflecting each time that for such a big house sounds did seem to carry awfully well, that the two of them seemed to rattle around in there. She heard the toaster popping up, and Michael putting it down again, and she turned over to go back to sleep.

In the kitchen, Michael was taking the butter and the honey down from the cupboard and waiting for the kettle to boil. The American woman appeared in the doorway – this was Michael's account of it, later – and said she hoped she wasn't interrupting but could she ask him something? Michael said yes, certainly, and she came into the room and sat down. Her situation was more complicated than she'd expected, she told him. It seemed she would have to go back to New York to get copies of her medical records, a referral from her doctor, her insurance documents. Which was a problem because she didn't have the money to go home and come back again. Michael asked if there wasn't someone she could get to send the documents. The woman looked at him, and ignored his interruption, telling him again that she didn't have that kind of money, not to go home and come back again. She didn't even have the money to get down to Heathrow, ha ha – this said as if it was all a big joke, according to Michael, or rather as if she wanted him to think that she was bravely trying to make it all into a big joke – and so she knew it was a lot to ask after all the kindness they'd already shown her but did Michael think there was any chance he could help out at all? Financially?

Michael told her he was sorry but he didn't think he could do that. Which seemed to surprise her, he said. Seemed to nudge her off-balance. Something in her expression changed, was the way he described it. But all she said was that she was sorry to have troubled him. And then, as they were both moving into the hallway, asking if she could ask him something else. A nod or a shrug from Michael, and she said that she'd noticed something was wrong, that she wondered if there were maybe some problems between him and his wife. And the answer heard by Catherine, as she stood in their bedroom doorway at the top of the stairs, was that he didn't think that was an appropriate question actually, ha ha; whereas the answer in the account he gave her later was a far less equivocal *no*.

He'd left for a meeting at the church then, and the American woman had gone back to her room, and she must have already started packing because by the time Catherine had been to the bathroom and washed her hair the woman had disappeared: the room empty, the sheets stripped, the front door key left on the bare mattress with a note.

She stood in the empty room for a few moments, feeling the blessed silence settle around her, and then she went downstairs to set the table for lunch. She scrubbed and pierced two jacket potatoes and put them in the oven. She washed and drained and mixed a salad, and made a dressing. She looked in the kitchen drawer where they kept their bank cards and passports and housekeeping money, and made sure everything was there. She checked that Michael's new laptop computer was still in the study. She ran the vacuum cleaner around the spare room, emptied the wastepaper basket of yoghurt pots, straightened the rug. She took the crumpled sheets downstairs and put them in the washing machine, and when she went back upstairs she checked through her jewellery box.

It wasn't that she'd thought the woman would turn out to be a thief. Not really. She just wanted some rational explanation for the way she'd felt about her, the suspicion and unease which she couldn't bring herself to admit might have been unfounded.

It felt like a long time before Michael got home. He started telling her about the meeting almost before he'd opened the door, tugging off his shoes in the hallway and rattling on about misplaced funding priorities and a dean who cared more about church buildings than putting the gospel into practice. She waited for him to finish talking before telling him that the woman was gone, by which time they were sitting at the table with a dressed salad and two steaming baked potatoes between them. She showed him the note the woman had left, unfolding it from her cardigan pocket and smoothing it out on the table. THANK YOU, it said, SEE YOU AGAIN SOON. He smiled, and nodded, and draped a napkin across his lap.

'What do you think she means?' Catherine asked. '*See you again soon?*'

'Oh, I'm sure it's nothing. Just a figure of speech.'

'Really?'

'Really.' He straightened the napkin on his lap, and fiddled with his knife and fork. 'Crisis over,' he said. He poured out two glasses of water. 'Did she take anything?'

'No. I looked, but I don't think anything's missing.'

'Did she say anything when she left, besides the note?'

'No, nothing.'

They shut their eyes and said a prayer of thanks and cut open their potatoes, the steam rushing out into the room and filling the space between them for a moment while they each waited for the other to reach for the butter and the salt.

'Well,' he said. He was almost smiling. He felt vindicated, she supposed. 'I imagine that's that then.'

'Yes,' she said. 'I imagine you do.'

The Chicken And The Egg

Stickford

It's not really something he likes talking abou
It is, in actual fact, quite a difficult thing to
it's becoming more of an issue. It's having kno
What it is, he has this fear of breaking ope
type of phobia. There doesn't seem to be a La
it. He's checked. But essentially he has this f
one day break open an egg and find a little b
foetus curled up inside. Dead. Occasionally h
being just about alive – *limply flopping* is the p
comes to mind – but he's pretty sure that's ju
irrational.

He is in actual fact quite sure the whole thin
but he can't get the idea out of his head. He b
thing about poultry-farming methods; he's b
into it, and he knows that the chances of a f
developed egg making its way into the ret
just about impossible. For starters if it was

more about church buildings than putting the gospel into practice. She waited for him to finish talking before telling him that the woman was gone, by which time they were sitting at the table with a dressed salad and two steaming baked potatoes between them. She showed him the note the woman had left, unfolding it from her cardigan pocket and smoothing it out on the table. THANK YOU, it said, SEE YOU AGAIN SOON. He smiled, and nodded, and draped a napkin across his lap.

'What do you think she means?' Catherine asked. '*See you again soon*?'

'Oh, I'm sure it's nothing. Just a figure of speech.'

'Really?'

'Really.' He straightened the napkin on his lap, and fiddled with his knife and fork. 'Crisis over,' he said. He poured out two glasses of water. 'Did she take anything?'

'No. I looked, but I don't think anything's missing.'

'Did she say anything when she left, besides the note?'

'No, nothing.'

They shut their eyes and said a prayer of thanks and cut open their potatoes, the steam rushing out into the room and filling the space between them for a moment while they each waited for the other to reach for the butter and the salt.

'Well,' he said. He was almost smiling. He felt vindicated, she supposed. 'I imagine that's that then.'

'Yes,' she said. 'I imagine you do.'

The Chicken And The Egg

Stickford

It's not really something he likes talking about, to be fair. It is, in actual fact, quite a difficult thing to discuss. But it's becoming more of an issue. It's having knock-on effects. What it is, he has this fear of breaking open eggs. It's a type of phobia. There doesn't seem to be a Latin name for it. He's checked. But essentially he has this fear that he'll one day break open an egg and find a little baby chicken foetus curled up inside. Dead. Occasionally he imagines it being just about alive – *limply flopping* is the phrase which comes to mind – but he's pretty sure that's just him being irrational.

He is in actual fact quite sure the whole thing's irrational but he can't get the idea out of his head. He knows something about poultry-farming methods; he's been looking into it, and he knows that the chances of a fertilised and developed egg making its way into the retail chain are just about impossible. For starters if it was an egg from a battery-cage site then it stands to reason it wouldn't be fertilised. Due to the cages, that would be. And even on the organic or free-range sites they do have these incredibly strict inspection regimes. It would be a failure of what he's been reliably informed are very robust systems. Millions and millions of eggs are produced every single day.

It would only take one.

It started when he overheard a man in a café describing it actually happening to him. The man was the owner of the café. He was talking to a woman at the counter who was ordering breakfast. He told her that some years previously, when he was working in the kitchen, he'd broken an egg and found a baby chicken inside. He described it in quite some detail, was the thing: how perfectly formed the foetus had been, with feathers and everything, how there was mostly blood and membrane where the yolk should have been. He told the woman it had quite shaken him up and he'd been unable to cook with eggs from then on. The woman changed her mind about what she was ordering. It's a conversation he can remember very clearly. There were certain shapes the man made with his hands while he was describing it all.

But when he knew it had got really bad was this one time when he was staying with his wife at a B&B. It was out in the country somewhere and the landlady kept chickens in the garden. His wife had liked that. She'd thought it was very authentic. Only he'd noticed that there was a rooster in with the hens, and then at breakfast he'd found these dark-red specks in the yolks of their fried eggs. Tiny specks, to be fair, about the size of a pencil mark made with a very sharp pencil. But he'd understood what they were. And the trouble was, he hadn't wanted to say anything to his wife, and he hadn't wanted to offend the landlady, and so he'd gone ahead and eaten the bloody things. And then what was awful was that they were absolutely delicious: they were literally the freshest eggs he'd ever eaten and they really were very good. Creamy and soft. Light. But at the same time he hadn't been able to stop thinking about the tiny dark-red specks. It was as if his imagination was a microscope, was the way he thought of it. And after that the whole trouble with eggs got serious, was what happened, was how he recalls it happening.

It's the anticipation which gets him. Even just thinking about it. Even nowhere near a cooking situation or an eating situation, just thinking about it at some other moment. The anticipation is what really does the damage. If he does happen to find himself in an unavoidable egg-breaking scenario, the tension is almost literally palpable. His stomach clenches, and his face more or less prepares to express disgust. He'll stand there with the egg held out at arm's length, like what it might do is explode. He'll close his eyes, and brace himself, and crack it into the bowl or the pan, and then once his eyes are shut what he has to do is brace himself all over again to open his eyes and look.

If it could just happen, is what he's started to think. If he could get it over and done with. Then he wouldn't be all worked up with the anticipation. The reality of it might not even be all that bad, considering. Considering all the things he's imagined.

Sometimes he's imagined it happening with a hard-boiled egg. Picking off the shell, getting the salt and pepper ready, and then cutting through the firm white of the egg and making the discovery. On a picnic. On a train. At a business meeting. Or even worse, having served the hard-boiled eggs to a guest. In a salad, such as perhaps a salad of cos lettuce and rocket, with a dusting of paprika across the eggs, some quarters of very ripe tomato, parmesan shavings, an olive-oil dressing. The eggs still just warm enough to release the fragrance of the olive oil. The guest being the first to cut into the egg.

Or also he's imagined it happening whilst preparing a fried-egg sandwich. The oil heating in the cast-iron pan. The thick slices of white bread lightly toasted, buttered, and dressed with tomato ketchup. The tea brewing in the pot. Breaking the egg into the pan, looking away for one moment to grab the salt and pepper and then turning back to find it there just as the white begins crackling at the edges. And what would happen then would be the heat having the effect of making the foetal chicken turn over in the pan, or just twitch slightly. It would create an illusion, is what he thinks.

And, yes, he understands there are effective treatments available for phobias. He has made some discreet enquiries, is how he knows this, and how he knows these treatments to be mostly based around a programme of gradually increasing exposure and reassurance. But then what it comes down to is he can't imagine how this would be any help at all. In his particular situation. Which isn't something he likes to discuss, to be fair. He has cracked open plenty of eggs in the course of his life, so whatever it is he needs to do it's not increasing his exposure, gradually or otherwise. Reassurance would be another thing. All these eggs he's cracked over the years and if anything the phobia is only getting worse. What he thinks is this is only logical. If the odds of it actually happening are one-in-a-million or one-in-a-billion or however high they are, then what follows is that with every egg he safely cracks open the probability actually increases. He's not sure if the statistical reasoning of this is entirely sound. But he still can't help feeling that every egg brings him closer to the thing he dreads.

So he did tell his wife about all this, eventually. He had to tell someone, was the conclusion he came to. It didn't help matters, as it turned out. She was what he would call notably unsympathetic. It could be said to have brought things to a head between them. There was some mockery. There was a poorly executed hoax involving a child's toy. Also, a man with whom he was vaguely acquainted at work, a man who was later identified as a co-respondent in the subsequent divorce proceedings, made a barely audible clucking noise as they stood together in the canteen line.

He hasn't actually discussed it with anyone else since then, to be fair. He's not at all sure it would help.

New York

New York

Okay. So there are these guys, these two guys, and they're standing by the side of the road, waiting for something. What are they waiting for? We don't know what they're waiting for. Not yet. That's part of the suspense, okay? Okay. So they're standing there, they're looking kinda tired, kinda downbeat, y'know? Yeah. Regular-looking, I guess. The one guy, he's older, he's sorta late-forties, early-fifties, getting a little thin on top. Big mustache. No, forget the mustache. But he hasn't had, like, a shave, not in a while. Okay. And the other guy, he's a bit younger, he's in his twenties, he's kinda good-looking but rough around the edges with it, y'know? Also, they've both got this kinda old European look about them, nothing obvious, not the mustache or anything but just enough that when they start talking we ain't surprised to hear they got these sorta like thick Polish accents, y'know? You with me? Right. Only they can't both have the Polish accents, otherwise how come they'd be talking in English at all, right? So let's say the younger guy it's more of a Slovak accent or something. I don't know. They got to have different enough accents that we accept them talking English when it's obvious they don't talk all that much English, y'know what I'm saying?

I told you already, New York. It's set in New York. Right.

So these two guys, they're standing by the side of the road and they're waiting for something. We don't know what they're waiting for but they're waiting. That's the fucken suspense right there. They both got bags with them, these little plastic dime-store bags, with like a lunch-sack and a flask of coffee and maybe some work-clothes in them. So they look like working men, okay? They look like they've been working all day. So we think maybe they've finished work and they're waiting for a ride home. And the camera pulls back a bit and we see a bunch of people waiting with them, same type of people, same clothes, bags, whatever, so we get a little context. But it's clear that these two guys are, y'know, the guys. And it's clear they've been waiting a while, because as the camera pulls back a bit more and we see the fields and farmhouses in the background we can see it's getting near that kinda summertime dusk that comes real late in the evening, like nine or ten in the evening. Five to ten, what-ever. Fucken magic hour.

Fields and farmhouses, right. Yeah, like I said already: New York, Lincolnshire. Right. Lincolnshire, England. They got the original New York right there. Little two-bit place. Coupla houses and a shop and a long straight road that goes all the way through to Boston. Right, Boston,

Lincolnshire. I told you this already. Flat fields. Bitter wind. Crows and shit in the trees. The works.

So. Anyway. We got these establishing shots: our two guys, the wider group, the empty fields, the skies and all that, right? So then we give it some of that testing-the-audience's-patience European-style time-passing, y'know what I mean, all that with the first he scratches his eyebrow, then he sniffs, then a tractor goes past real slow. All that. To establish the mood! To make sure the audience knows these guys are tired as all shit, and get them wondering what's with the waiting. Okay? And then we're into the dialogue. This piece is all about the dialogue, you with me? So first up the one guy goes, 'It's cold.' Right? And we just had a location caption saying, 'New York,' so we're kinda making the connection ourselves and hearing it as 'New York, it's cold.' Right. You with me? That ring any bells for you? Okay, so then they talk about the weather a little bit, and what time it is, and then they start bitching about how the supervisor or whoever is taking so long coming back with the mini-van to pick them all up and take them back to their place of residence. And the one guy says something about him never being early. And the other guy says how he's always late. You getting this yet? No? They're waiting for their van, right? Van, man, whatever. We get right into the dialogue and they're all talking about how hard the day's been, like picking whatever it is they've been picking in the field all day long, like cabbages or something, I don't know, onions and celery and all that, some real back-breaking dawn-till-dusk shit and now the supervisor has left them stranded while he's all off down in the village or whatever. The

village. Right. Exactly. You're with me now. So they're talking about how they're sick of it, the working conditions,
the money, all that. And the audience get to wondering
about the dialogue, like how come it sounds so awkward
and disjointed, and like, all right already so these guys are
foreign but that don't really explain it, there's something
else going on, something kinda funny, and some of these
lines sound kinda familiar. All right. So the younger guy's
doing most of the bitching, but the older guy, he's the wise
one, he's giving it all that you-do-what-you-gotta-do, and
the younger guy's not having it so he gets to saying that's it,
that's enough already, he's out of there, he's leaving today.
And then the audience are like, right, now we get it. Okay?
You with me? They don't got no words of their own, they're
just saying all this second-hand shit they heard on the
radio, and they're making us think of the new New York,
the one we all know about, the one which is, like, built on
immigration and exploitation and the hard fucken labour
of the huddled masses like our two friends right here.

Fucken I don't know, Wiktor and Andrej. Whatever.
Right.

So they keep talking, and we're still with the Euro-style
fucken *longueurs* and like meaningful glances and shit.
Y'know. Old man rides past on a bike, real slow. Birds
rise up from the trees and circle round and settle back in
the trees. All these long pauses, like, signifying the passing of time. Because they're waiting for this ride back to
their residence, right? And the one guy, he's still talking
about how he's sick of this work and the money and everything and he'd rather be back home, and the older guy's

110

all, like: there's no work back home! What would you do? You'd be walking the streets drinking knock-off vodka and getting ripped off by the cops! Y'know, basically the same shit migrant workers have always talked about. But still, everything they're saying is like lines we've heard before, y'know? One of them says he's going if he has to walk, the other one says something about it not being that far, the one of them goes he came looking for a job. All that. And we're taking it like a game now, this is we the audience I mean, like trying to recognise shit. But then we're thinking, well, hold up now, this don't make no sense. How come these guys don't got their own words for these things? How come they're talking all this borrowed shit? Right? So then we get to thinking, wait a minute now, so maybe the joke's on us. Maybe we're hearing all this second-hand clichéd stuff because we can't really hear what these guys are saying. We see them standing at the side of the road and we're like, right, yeah, we know this one, migrant labourers, tired and weary, getting paid shit, getting ripped off, taking it in turns to sleep in the same bed, sending money home, the engine room of the modern economy, all that headline crap. But we don't know shit. We really don't know. So if we were to stop and listen to them talking for a minute, we wouldn't even hear what they were saying anyhow. This is the fucken point which is being elaborated before the audience's very eyes, y'know?

I mean, talk to me about appropriation, right? The city don't even got its own name! And here are these two guys standing in the original New York! Y'know?

Right. Anyway. So. Meanwhile it's pretty much dark,

and our two guys are still standing there. They smoke a cigarette, they drink a bit of coffee from the flask, some kids drive past and shout some kinda nasty shit at them. All that. And while we're getting the hang of all this the-joke's-on-us kinda stuff, we don't hardly notice that they've started talking about some friend of theirs, this other migrant guy who's died in a like tragic fire at some other place of residence, and how are they going to get to the funeral, and what clothes can they wear, and does anyone even know how to get word to his family. Right? And by the time we do notice, they've quit talking about it anyway. So that's another twist for the audience right there: how is it we were too busy thinking about the meaning of what's going on with the dialogue to even notice that these two guys were having some individualistic shitty fucken narrative in their own lives? Which just goes to prove the point, right? Well, it do, don't it?

So. Anyway, that's about it right there. Yeah. Their ride never shows up. They pour out some more coffee and the one guy spits it out and goes, 'Is cold.' That being the first line of dialogue we heard, meaning they're trapped in some kinda Beckettian loop or whatever. Yeah. We fade out and roll credits or whatever.

Of course it's fucken conceptual. What do I look like to you?

Slipway

SUTTON
ON SEA

French Tea

Sutton-on-Sea

I was wiping tables. It was quiet. We hadn't done many
lunches, and they were all gone. There was only that
woman in, with a tea. She was talking on, the way she does.
I could see the floor needed mopping but I didn't think I
could do it while she was there. There was a swell on the
sea, and a rainstorm passing over to the south. You could
see the windmills really going for it, catching the light from
somewhere. The only people out on the beach were the
ones walking their dogs. She was saying how that was a
proper pot of tea I'd made her. Going on the way she does.
The usual about how you don't always get a proper pot of
tea these days, and how some places they don't even use a
pot. 'Just dump the bag straight in the mug and expect you
to fish it out yourself,' she says. 'Not like this,' she says.
'This is a proper pot of tea.' It's never even that clear who
she thinks she's talking to. I give her a nod or a smile now
and again but that only seems to confuse her, so mostly I

115

let her get on with it. It's not like she's not said all this about the tea before. I could probably have said most of it word for word.

'I went to London once,' she says, 'and this young man made me a tea using the water from a coffee machine, a coffee machine, I couldn't believe it, he used the hot water from a coffee machine and filled up one of those bowl-shaped mugs, hot water mind you, it wasn't even boiling, it was hot water, and he put the tea-bag on the saucer and just left it sitting there.' I was doing the condiments by then. Most people take that as a hint but she doesn't. I collected up all the salt and pepper pots and checked them over. 'The water getting colder and colder and the tea-bag just sitting there on the saucer doing absolutely no good to anyone, and there's me standing at the counter watching him,' she says. I took all the lids off the tomatoes and topped up the ketchup. She was getting a bit heated. It was usually about now that other people would notice, if they were in, and start moving away. She says, 'I told him, I said do you mind, could you please, please put the tea-bag into the water, please, what on earth are you doing, are you making me a cup of French tea there?'

She more or less said that all in one go. It got her quite out of breath. It usually does. She said about the young man asking her what French tea was, and how she'd told him that in England we make tea with boiling water and we make damn well sure the water stays hot and that whatever it was he was doing it looked like something they'd do on the Continent. 'I went to France once,' she says. She looked out the window when she said it, peering over the sea as if she could see land. She said she went on a day trip there, and that was how they made their tea, and she didn't much care for it. There were some other things she didn't much care for but she didn't go into details. Or at least she did, but she mumbled them under her breath, as if they were too shameful to say out loud.

All the dishes were done by then, and the condiments. I was wiping over the menus. The wind must have changed direction. The rain came up the beach and against the windows. I could see the dog-walkers making a run for it. One of them came charging in the door and I had to tell him to leave the dog outside. He just stood there without ordering anything, dripping on the floor. I was glad I hadn't done the mopping. The woman carried on talking, and I could tell he was trying to work out if she was talking to him or not. He figured it out soon enough. 'I've never bothered going back, I'm not much of a one for travelling,' she says. 'What's the point of going away? You only have to come back.'

The man didn't really know where to look, I could tell. I told him the rain would blow over soon enough and he nodded.

'All these people jetting off all over the place,' the woman said, still rattling on. 'I don't know what they think they're going to find. It's all the same. People are the same. And you can't get a decent cup of tea. Not for love nor money. This is a decent cup of tea. In a pot. Proper china. Fresh milk. It's not rocket science. But that man just stood there looking at me, asking me what I meant, and all the while the tea-bag was just sitting on the saucer and the water was getting colder and colder. I ask you. Really.'

The rain stopped and the man went out. His dog came bounding over and shook all the water off while the door was still open, so that went all over the floor. I went and put the door on the catch, and turned the boilers off, and started cashing up.

'Take my daughter,' she says. 'She's off working in some country or other. Doesn't seem to have broadened her mind. She's been gone nearly a year now and she's barely even written. Don't even rightly know where she is. And you can bet your bottom dollar she's not getting a decent cup of tea. This is a decent cup of tea. This is a proper cup of tea. This is what you want to expect when you ask for a tea. A pot and a jug and some good china. It's important to know what to expect. You expect to get what you expect. You don't get that when you go away. You don't know what to expect. Leaving the bag on the saucer like that, with the water going cold. And you only have to come back.'

The sun was out for a minute, and the sea was shining, but there was another shower coming in. I started filling the mop bucket, and turned a couple of chairs over. She started getting all her bags together. She shook her head a few times, as if she was annoyed with something.

'Listen to me going on,' she said. The way she says it, it sounds like that's really what she means. What she wants. But I had things to be getting on with.

Close

Gainsborough

She wouldn't tell Patricia. She'd decided that before even saying goodbye, before she'd stood there and listened to his footsteps crunch away through the gravel. What was there to tell anyway. It was only talking.

And he'd approached her first. When they were standing in the reception room, holding their information leaflets and waiting for the tour of the Imperial Palace to begin. You're English right, he'd said, and she'd nodded, and he'd asked if they might swap cameras for the morning, for the duration of the tour. Which she hadn't understood straight away. He wanted his picture taken, he'd explained, with his camera, and he wanted to return the favour. Which was no sort of favour at all because she didn't like being in her own holiday photos. She knew what she looked like.

It'll save us swapping back and forth every time, he'd said.

It had seemed rude to say no, once he'd asked. And there had been other people standing there, other people he could have asked, but he'd asked her. Which was something.

He was in Japan for three weeks, he'd told her. Tokyo, Kyoto, Osaka. The whole *shebang*. Spending his army pension, because he figured what the hey it's just sitting there and he happened to have this time on his hands. He was *between jobs*, he said, smiling in a way which was surprising for such a big man. Boyish was the word she thought of, although she didn't think he was any younger than her. Ex-US Army Engineers, so he'd seen a few countries in his time but had never been to Japan, always wanted to. Been working in a repair shop the last few years, welding, but the work had dried up. Living in Duluth, Minnesota, which when you figured all the countries he'd been through it was funny how it wasn't a million miles from where he'd started out. Good place to be, and it was handy for where his kids lived now.

He'd told her all this before the tour had even started, and in return she'd told him that she was a school secretary from Gainsborough, Lincolnshire – like the artist, she'd said, although it's no oil painting, and she'd been surprised when he laughed – and that she was only here for a week. He'd done more of the talking, it was fair to say.

And when they'd introduced themselves, just as the tour began, he'd held out his hand for her to shake. Which she hadn't been expecting. He had a very large hand. He was really quite a large man, he looked sort of like a rugby player or something and she could see even from where she was standing that none of it was fat. Shaking hands with him had made her feel sort of petite. Which she certainly wasn't used to.

Wade, he'd said. Elizabeth, she'd replied.

That room though. If they were going to have that many people waiting in there for the tours to begin, they should have had a fan or something. Air-conditioning. It was too hot, really. Close.

He'd asked her to take the first picture almost immediately, as the group was walking across the great expanse of white gravel, the crunch of their footsteps swallowed up by the hot, still air. He'd been asking where else she was visiting while she was here, if she'd been out of Kyoto at all, and she'd said yes, there were day trips organised as part of the package she was on: to Nara, Himeji, Hiroshima. She'd felt awkward mentioning Hiroshima, as if he might have felt some kind of association. Oh yeah, he'd said, I went to Hiroshima, day before last. That was something else. *Awesome*. And he'd made this long, loud sigh, as if he was trying to clear stale air from his lungs. Not really a fun trip, but you kind of have to, he'd said, looking at her. Waiting for her agreement, which she'd happily given, nodding and saying oh absolutely I think so. Which was when he'd looked round at the first of the palace buildings and suggested getting a picture right there, standing and framing himself against it while she lifted his camera to her face.

And if she does tell someone about this when she gets home, not Patricia but someone at least, she'll say that this was when she first noticed, properly, what he looked like.

There was the moustache, of course, and the sheer solid size of the man. But there was something else, something soft and quiet in his face and his eyes, something that contrasted with his loud talk and his oversized hands. It was nice, looking at him like that through the viewfinder.

They'd changed places then, as the rest of the group moved away, and she'd felt her already flushed face colour further as he'd looked at her through her camera, and wished she'd been wearing a different outfit. Something cooler. Something less pink. And something other than that pair of trousers. Patricia had told her before that they didn't work – they don't do anything to help with your size is all I'm saying, she'd said, the only time Elizabeth had worn them in the office – but she'd got up in a hurry that morning and they were the first thing that had come to hand, and the whole outfit had looked nice in the air-conditioned hotel room, had looked cool and elegant and English-roseish. But now, standing for a picture she didn't want taken anyway, she just felt hot, and pink, and fat. And so why did she even think he might have been interested. She wasn't seventeen any more. Not by a long way.

The tour guide had already started by the time they'd caught up with the rest of the group. His Imperial Majesty would arrive from long journey in ox-drawn carriage, she was saying, pronouncing *ox-der-awn-car-riage* very precisely, as if it was essential that they understood. She described the entrance building behind her, with its low flight of steps and receding series of empty rooms lined with painted silk screens and tatami-mat floors.

She'd felt Wade nudging her. How d'you find life in Gainsborrow? he'd whispered. She'd been a bit embarrassed that he was talking while the guide was talking, but still.

It's Gains*borough*, she'd whispered back, and he'd put his hand over his mouth and made an apologetic face, which was nice that he thought it was important. Sorry, he'd whispered; how's life in *Gains-bor-ough*, splitting the word up the way the tour guide had done with ox-drawn carriage, which was maybe a bit mean but very funny as well the way he did it, and so then it had been her turn to put her hand over her mouth, to hide her laughter. It's not bad, she'd said, it's not the centre of the universe but it's a nice place to live. He'd held up his hands when she'd said that. Hey, he'd whispered, we can't all live in the centre of the universe, can we? It'd be a bit crowded if we did; and that had made her laugh again, and this time one or two people had turned around to look.

They'd clicked very quickly, that was the thing. That was something else that was new.

So, the guide had said then; please now to the *Oi-ke-ni-wa* Garden. And everyone had turned and followed her across the gravel, except that by some silent agreement Wade and Elizabeth had waited and lagged a short way behind.

Wade and Elizabeth. It had a ring to it, but what was she thinking.

She'd asked him if he liked living in Minnesota, and he'd said, sure it was fine, it was home, and he'd mentioned again that it was good to be near to his kids. He'd asked her if she enjoyed being a school secretary, and she'd said she supposed there were worse jobs she could be doing. He'd laughed, and said that was true enough, and she'd asked about his children. You mentioned your children were nearby, she'd said: are they at university or something? Surprising herself even as she said it, because she didn't always find small talk easy but this time she had. Which had made her think.

He'd looked at her, and she'd realised straight away that she'd missed the point. No, he'd said, they're too young for that just yet. They're living with their mother.

She could have died. Right there. Really.

Oh, she'd said. I'm sorry. I didn't think.

No, it's okay, he'd said. It was a while ago now. These things happen, you know how it is. He'd made a face, a sort of knowing frown, as if to say I'd rather not go into details but I'm sure you can guess. She wasn't sure that she could. The thing kind of got out of hand in the end, he'd said. The moment had kind of passed. She nodded slowly, in a way which she hoped looked like sympathetic recognition. You got children? he asked.

No, she said, no I haven't.

He looked like he was waiting for her to add something, but she didn't. Because what would she have said. Because what else was there to say.

The other people on the tour had all been younger than her and Wade, and she'd wondered how it was that young people these days seemed able to travel anywhere in the world that took their fancy. This was just one holiday

124

among many for them, and the ones who didn't know each other already were asking about it; none of them saying *where you from?*, she noticed, but rather *where you been?* and *where you headed?* One of them, a tall American girl in a sleeveless top and a pair of sensible walking shorts, all long brown limbs and neat blonde hair, had turned to Wade and said *hey how's it going,* as the tour guide led them through the garden to the next talking point, and Wade had said *hey, good, thanks* in reply. Leaving Elizabeth a bit stranded as they started a conversation of their own.

It was a beautiful garden. There was a lake, a large pond really, with a low arched bridge at one end, and a pebbled shore, and a stream winding down towards it from a stand of bamboo. There were the usual clipped and twisted trees, and carefully placed rocks, and mossy seating areas. The whole garden felt natural and artificial at the same time, and she wondered if there were hidden meanings to the arrangement which you were meant to decode. She'd wanted to say something to Wade about it, but he'd still been talking to that girl, asking her where the best temples in Cambodia were – the girl had been to Cambodia, of course – and she couldn't catch his eye. She'd waited for them to finish their conversation, and when she'd realised she'd been standing there too long she'd moved away a little, looking at the bridge on the far side of the lake, looking at the tour guide, looking at the palace buildings and the other people in the group. Because it didn't matter if he wanted to talk to someone else. Because why would that matter to her. She stood off to one side, holding his camera, waiting. Like some sort of she didn't know what. Spear-carrier. Spare part.

That girl though. It must be sunny all the time where she was from, judging by how tanned those long slim limbs were, the carefree freckles on her face. She must have never lost a night's sleep over anything, she'd thought, and been surprised by her own bitterness. Because was this who she'd become, already. She tried to remember, and she couldn't, when she'd last been able to wear shorts, or anything without sleeves.

What sort of a name was *Wade* anyway, she'd found herself thinking.

So, please, the guide had said then; please, this is *Oh-ga-ku-mon-jo*. In festival times poetry recitals would be held here, she'd said, and gestured towards a painted silk screen in an open room behind her. The painting showed a group of finely dressed courtiers sitting cross-legged in a garden, and the guide had explained that this was the garden they were standing in now. If you look, these courtiers are sitting beside stream, she'd said; and this is same stream here, with same group of three rocks also.

She just didn't know her way around this sort of thing, was the problem. She wasn't familiar with the territory. She couldn't read the situation, if there was ever a situation to read. Patricia had told her once that she was better off without a man, that she couldn't imagine the trouble they caused. Elizabeth assumed she'd meant well, but she really hadn't appreciated it. She'd said, Patricia, if I want your opinion on my private life I'll ask and until then I'd rather not have that sort of comment thank you. Which Patricia hadn't responded to, but when she'd refilled the paper tray on the photocopier she'd slammed it so hard that Elizabeth had been surprised it didn't break.

At these poetry recitals there was a particular tradition, the guide had continued, gesturing towards the painted screen again; there would be small cups of sake in folded paper boats floating down from the top of the stream. And aim was to invent short poem on given subject before boat reaches you, she said; if you could not think of poem quickly enough then you were not permitted to drink sake, you must allow boat to pass by.

Which would be enough to make you never want to go to a garden party again, she'd thought. Being put on the spot like that. Watching the little paper boat wobble past you and not being able to think of a thing to say. Because it would feel sort of exposed, something like that.

The tour guide had smiled then, and asked if there were any questions, and led the group off towards the last point of the tour. Elizabeth had hung back for a moment, looking at the painted screen, the four figures seated on the moss around the stream. They were so plump it was difficult to see if they were men or women: their long black hair coiled around their heads, their kimonos folded richly around them. They didn't look nervous. They didn't look as if they'd have trouble thinking of something witty and poetic in the short time they had, reciting their lines, reaching out to take the cup before the paper boat had passed them, before it folded and crumpled into the water and the sake spilt away downstream.

*   *   *

Wade had been waiting for her at the exit, smiling. I was starting to worry about you, he said. Which, she hadn't known what to say to that. And then he'd said, so, I guess that's us, isn't it?

Yes, she said. I suppose it is.

He'd lowered his head to take her camera from round his neck, and for a moment she'd thought he was bowing in the traditional Japanese style, and she'd started to bow in return before she'd realised he wasn't at all. And she was sure he'd noticed, but he didn't say anything. Which stuck in her mind, because some people would have laughed at her right there. But he didn't laugh. He shook her hand again, and said goodbye, and see you around, and take care, and then he kept talking. He asked if she was going straight back to work when she got home, what she wanted to do if she didn't want to be a secretary for ever, and she said I don't know, teach? Which had been funny somehow. She asked him how long he thought he'd be between jobs for, if he was planning to stay in Minnesota. I think I will, he said, I feel like it's where I belong now. It's beautiful country round there, he said, and she'd been surprised by the feeling with which he'd said it; had tried to imagine ever feeling that way about Gainsborough or Lincolnshire or anywhere she lived. You ever been? he asked. To the States? she said. No, to Minnesota, he said, to Duluth, and she smiled and said, well anyway no, neither. You should come over sometime, he said. You'd like it.

Which was when Patricia would say she should have said something, just then. When she got home and told her

128

about it. But she said nothing, only goodbye and take care and see you around.

And she decided, as she stood in the deep green shade of a cypress tree and listened to his footsteps crunch away along the gravelled path, to go back and have another look at the palace garden. She wanted to get a picture of the stream, and the rocks, and the small stand of bamboo trees. If she was quick she could get back in before the palace guides closed up, before they locked the gates and put out the No Entry signs and asked her to come back and try again another day.

We Wave And Call

Wainfleet

And sometimes it happens like this: a young man lying face down in the ocean, his limbs hanging loosely beneath him, a motorboat droning slowly across the bay, his body moving in long, slow ripples with each passing shallow wave, the water moving softly across his skin, muffled shouts carrying out across the water, and the electric crackle of waves sliding up against the rocks and birds in the trees and the body of a young man lying in the ocean, face down and breathlessly still.

*

You open your eyes, blinking against the light which pulses through the water. You look down at the sea floor, hearing only the hollow suck and sigh of your own breath through the snorkel, seeing the broken shells, the rusting beer cans, the polished pieces of broken glass. Black-spiked sea-urchins clinging to the rocks. Tiny black fish moving through the sea-grass. A carrier-bag tumbling in tight circles at the foot of the shoreline rocks. You hold out your hands, seeing how pale they look in the water, the skin of your fingers beginning to pucker a little. The sea feels as warm as bath-water, and you're almost drifting off to sleep when you hear the sudden smack and plunge of something hitting the water nearby.

You turn your head, and see a young boy sinking through the water, his knees to his chest and his eyes squeezed shut. Above, way up in the air, another three boys are falling from a high rocky outcrop, their shorts ballooning out around their hips, their hair rising, their mouths held open in anticipatory cries. One of them flaps his hands, trying to slow his fall. The other two reach out and touch the tips of their fingers together. All three of them look down at the water with something like fear and joy.

Your friends are watching as well, sprawled across a wide concrete ledge jutting out over the sea. Claire turns and looks for you, waving, brushing the knots from her wet tangled hair. Her pale skin is shiny with sun-cream and seawater.

'We're making a move now,' she calls; 'you coming?'

The others are already standing up, brushing bits of dirt from their skin and shaking out their towels. You lift the mask from your face and take the snorkel from your mouth and tell her you're staying in a bit longer. You'll catch them up in a minute, you say.

They pick up the sun-cream and water bottles, the paperback books, the leaflets from the tourist information office in town. The girls lift up their damp hair, squeezing out the water and letting it run down their backs. Andy buttons his shirt and steps into his unlaced trainers.

'We're not waiting for you,' Claire says. You wave her off and say that's fine. You'll be out in a minute or two.

The night before, sitting at a table outside one of the cafés in the old town, the girls had got up to go to the toilet together, leaving their tall glasses of beer on the table and tugging at their skirts. Andy had caught your eye, and lifted his drink in salute, and you'd both smiled broadly at your good fortune. Nothing had needed to be said. You'd left behind long months of exams and anxieties in the flat grey east of England and landed suddenly in this new world of cheap beer and sunshine, of clear blue seas and girls who wore bikinis and short skirts and slept in the room next door. It felt like something you'd both been waiting years for; something you've long been promised. It felt like adulthood. The girls have already made it clear, by their pointing out of waiters and boys on scooters, that they're more interested in the locals than in the two of you. But there's still a chance. A feeling that something could happen; that anything could happen. It seems worth thinking about, at least.

You put the mask over your eyes and lie back in the water for a while, looking up at the steep sides of the bay, kicking your legs to send yourself drifting away from the rocks. You're not sure you ever want to get out. At home, the beach is a few minutes away, and you've grown up running in and out of the sea. But you've never really swum; there, you run in, shouting against the shock of the cold, and run out again as soon as you can. Here, you could sleep in the clear warm water. You watch the others making their way up the path between the pine trees and oleander bushes. A bus drives along the road at the top of the hillside, stops near the gap in the railings, and moves off. A young couple on a scooter overtake it, the boy riding without a shirt or a helmet, the girl wearing a knee-length wraparound skirt and a bikini top, her hair flowing out behind her. Birds hang still in the warm currents of air drifting up the side of the hill. The grasshoppers sound out their steady scraping shriek. The air is thick with the scent of crushed pine needles and scorched rosemary, heavy with heat.

Along the bay, at the bottom of a steep flight of steps cut straight from the rock, there's another small bathing jetty. A girl in a black swimming costume sits on the edge, her feet in the water, a white towel hanging over her head, reading a book.

Further along, where the bay curves round to form a long headland jutting out into the sea, there's an ugly concrete hotel with its name spelt out in white skyline letters. Half the letters are missing, and when you look again you see that the whole building is a ruin: the windows shot to pieces, gaping holes blown in the walls, coils of barbed wire rolling across the golden sands. Shreds of curtain material hang limply from windows and patio doors, lifting and dropping in the occasional breeze.

You hear some girls screaming, and look round to see a group of boys soaking them with water bottles, laughing when the girls scramble to their feet and retaliate with flat stinging hands. The sounds carry softly across the water.

You'd seen a map, this morning, at the entrance to the city walls, marked with clusters of red dots. The red dots were to show where mortar shells had landed during the war, where fires had started, where roofs had come crashing in. It was the only sign you could see, at first, that anything had happened here. Everything in the town seemed neat and clean and smooth: the streets polished to a shine, the ancient stonework unaffected by the destruction which had so recently poured down upon it. But when you'd looked closer you'd seen that the famous handmade roof tiles had been outnumbered by replacements in a uniform orange-red, and that the stonework of the historic city walls alternated between a weathered grey and the hard white gleam of something new. There were whole streets boarded off from the public, piled with rubble. There were buildings whose frontages had been cleaned and repaired but which were still gutted behind the shutters. And in a tiny court-yard workshop, under the shade of a tall lemon tree, you'd seen a fat-shouldered stonemason carving replica cornices and crests, the shattered originals laid out in fragments in front of him, glancing over his shoulder as if to be sure that no one could see. You'd wondered how long it would take for this rebuilding to be complete. How much longer it would take for the new stones to look anything like the old.

The others are halfway up the hill now, walking slowly along the pine-needled path, letting their hands trail through the sweet-smelling bushes, stopping for a drink of water and looking down at the calm shining sea. You watch them for a moment. You wave, but none of them sees. You call. If you were to get out now you might be able to catch up with them before they get on the bus. But if you wait for the next bus, they'll have cleared up by the time you get back, and got some food ready, and be waiting for you. Jo went out to the market before lunch, so the apartment's small kitchen is well stocked. You can imagine arriving back to find the others sitting on the terrace around a table loaded with food: bread and cheese and oranges, olives and pickles and jam, big packets of paprika-flavoured crisps. You can imagine cracking open a beer and joining them, making plans for the night.

You turn your face into the water for one more look before you get out, sucking in warm air through the snorkel. You catch sight of a larger fish than the ones you've seen so far. Something silver-blue, twice the length of your hand, drifting slowly between the rocks. It flicks its tail and glides away, and you push back with your legs to glide after it, trying not to splash. It slows again, leaning down to nibble at the wavering tips of seaweed, and as it flicks into another glide you follow, watching from above, quietly kicking your legs to keep pace.

And you think about last night. About what might have happened with Jo. Walking between the café and the bus stop, the alleys crowded, the buildings still giving out the heat of the day, the dark sky overhead squeezed between window-boxes and washing lines and women leaning out to smoke and look down at the crowds below. You lost sight of the others for a while, and then Jo was there, saying something, touching two fingers against your chest, letting one finger catch in the opening of your shirt. What did she say? It could have been nothing. The whole thing might have been nothing. But there were her fingers against your chest. That smile and turn. Walking behind her, and all the side-alleys and courtyards that might have been ducked into. And then catching up with the others at the bus stop, and nothing more being said.

You watch the fish flick its tail beneath you, stopping and starting through the sea-grass, and you curl your body across the surface to keep pace, the sun hot and sore across your back.

It happened once, last year, at a party after the exams. In the back garden, kissing against the wall of the house, and for what must have been only a few minutes there was nothing but the taste of her mouth, the movements of her hands, the press of her body. And then she'd stopped, and kissed you on the cheek, and walked unsteadily into the house, and nothing had been said about it since. It might have been nothing.

The soft wet bite of her lips, the trace of her fingers, the thin material of her skirt in your hand, the weight of her warmth against you. It was probably nothing at all.

You look up out of the water, turning to see if she's reached the top of the path. Maybe she'll hang back and wait. You're further out than you realised. It would be good to head back now, to pull yourself up on to the concrete ledge, let the sun dry the water from your back while you gather your things together and hurry along the path to join the others. You pull your arms through the water, feeling the pleasant stretch of the muscles across your shoulders and back. You kick with your legs, hard, and your feet and shins slap against the surface, and you realise how long it's been since you last swam properly like this, actually covering a distance. You should do it more often, you think, stopping for a moment to tuck the snorkel into the headband of your mask, spitting out a mouthful of seawater. You launch off again, enjoying the way your body cuts through the water, the air on your back, the sea sliding across your skin. The snorkel slips out of place, spilling water into your mouth, and you have to stop again, coughing, to clear it from your throat.

You see the others on the path, and you see a bus passing along the road, and you see the birds hanging in the warm air rising up against the side of the hill.

You take off the snorkel and mask. They're getting in the way, and you'll get back to the steps quicker without them strapped to your face. You try swimming with them held in one hand, but they slap and splash against the surface and drag you down, and you're not getting anywhere like that so you stop and tread water for a moment. You're further out than you thought.

The afternoon's quieter now. No one's jumped from the outcrop for a while. The teenagers on the ledge have started to gather their things together and drift back up the long twisting path to the road. The girl reading a book on the other bathing jetty has gone. The back of your neck feels as though it might be starting to burn. It probably would be good, after all, to catch the bus with the others. You think about just dumping the snorkel and mask, but it seems a bit over the top. There's nothing like that happening here. There's no problem. You can't be more than a hundred, maybe a hundred and fifty yards from the shore. You tie them to the drawstring of your swimming shorts instead, and swim on.

This morning, in the old town, ducking into an art gallery to escape the glaring heat, you'd found the city's war memorial, unmarked on the tourist maps. It had looked like another room of the gallery at first, and you'd drifted into the circular space expecting more vividly coloured paintings of wheat-fields and birch-woods and simple peasant-folk labouring over ploughs. But there were no paintings, only photographs. Black and white photographs from ceiling to floor. Row after row of young faces with dated haircuts, thin moustaches, leather jackets and striped tracksuit tops. The photos were blown up to more than life-size, and one or two had the inky smudge of a passport stamp circled across them. There were names, and dates, and ages: twenty-two, fifty-seven, fifteen, nineteen, thirty-one. There were candles burning on a table in the middle of the room, a bouquet of flowers, a ragged flag. Some of the boys in the photographs had looked the same age, and had the same features, as these teenagers jumping from rocks and squirting water at girls, boys who would have been half the age they are now when the war happened. You wonder if any of them lost older brothers, cousins, uncles, fathers. You wonder whether any of them remember much about it; if they duck into that cool, whitewashed room every now and again to remind themselves, or if they prefer instead to leap from high rocks into the warm ocean, to ride motor-scooters with the sun browning their bare chests, to lie with long-limbed girls in the scented shade of aged and twisting trees.

Perhaps when you get back no one will want to go to the trouble of laying the food out on the terrace and clearing it all away again. Perhaps you'll all go to the pizzeria down by the dockside and sit at a table on the street, picking the labels off cold bottles of beer while you watch the old women offering accommodation to the tourists coming off the boats. Perhaps Jo will catch your eye and keep you talking until the others have moved on, and shift her chair so that her leg touches yours.

Swimming with the mask and snorkel tied to your shorts is worse than holding them. They're dragging out between your legs like an anchor, pulling you back. You stop and tread water again, breathing heavily. You only paid a few pounds for them. They can go. You can always tell the others you left them behind by mistake. You unpick the knots and let them fall away. They hang in the water for a moment, lifting and turning in the current. You watch them sink out of view, and realise you can't see the bottom.

The others are at the top of the path now, and one of them leans out to look down at the ledge where your things are still gathered in a heap. You wave, but whoever it is turns away and steps through the gap in the railings, crossing the road to join the others at the bus stop, out of sight.

You take a breath and swim, fiercely, lunging through the water, blinking against the salt sting, heaving for air, and there's a feeling running up and down the backs of your legs like the muscles being stretched tight but you keep swimming because you'll be there soon, climbing out, pulling yourself back on to solid ground, and you keep swimming because there's a chance that the current has been pushing you away from the shore, and you keep swimming because this isn't the sort of thing that happens to someone like you, you're a good swimmer, you're young, and healthy, and the rocks aren't really all that far away and it shouldn't take long to get there and there isn't anything else you can do but now there's a pounding sensation in your head and a reddish blur in your eyes and a heavy pain in your chest as though the weight of all that water is pressing against your lungs and you can't take in enough air and so you stop again, for a moment, just to catch your breath.

One of the boys, in the memorial photographs, had had a look in his eyes. Startled. As though the flash of the camera had taken him by surprise. As though he had known what was coming. The plaque said he was seventeen. You wondered what had happened. If he really had seen it coming. You've seen pictures of an old fort on a nearby island, the walls spotted with bullet marks, the entrances surrounded by shallow craters, and you imagined that boy crouching on the roof, or in the shaded interior, holding an old rifle in his shaking hands, listening to the encircling approach of men and equipment through the trees and bushes outside. You imagined him listening to their taunts. Wiping the sweat from his eyes. Avoiding the glances of the men left with him. Wondering how they had all ended up in that place, what they could have done to avoid it, what they were going to do now. Knowing there was nothing they could do.

A bus stops on the road at the top of the hill. The others must be getting on it by now, rummaging in their pockets for change and wondering how much longer you're going to be. When you get back they'll all be sitting out on the terrace, watching the yachts gathering in the harbour for the evening, listening to children playing up and down the back streets behind the apartment. You'll take a beer from the fridge, hold the cold wet glass against the back of your sunburnt neck, and ask where the bottle-opener is. No one will be able to find it at first, and then it will turn up, under a book or a leaflet, or in the sink with some dirty plates, and you'll flip the top off the bottle and take your seat with the others.

You swim some more, and there's a feeling in your arms and legs as though the muscles have been peeled out of them, as though the bones have softened from being in the water too long, and you can't find the energy to pull yourself forward at all.

You turn on to your back for a few moments. A rest is all you need. It's been a while since you swam in open water like this, that's all. A few moments' rest and you'll be able to swim to the rocks, to the steps, and climb out. You'll be able to hang a towel over your pounding head until you get your breath back, dripping water and sweat on to the sunbleached concrete, feeling the warm solid ground beneath you. You'll be able to gather your things and make your

141

way along the path, pulling on your shirt as you go. And the grasshoppers will still be calling out, and the air will be thick with rosemary and pine. The sandy soil of the path will still kick up into dusty clouds around your ankles. Your swimming trunks will be dry by the time you get to the top of the hill, and you won't have to wait long for a bus. And while you stand there the sea will be as calm and blue as ever when you look down over it, drifting out to the horizon, reaching around to other bays, other beaches, other villages and towns, other swimmers launching out into its warm and gentle embrace.

And this will be a story to tell when you get back home, sitting under the patio-heaters at the Golf Club bar, looking out over the cold North Sea and saying it was a nice holiday but I nearly never made it home. Or later this evening, sitting at some pavement café in a noisy bustling square with tall glasses of cold beer, telling the story of how you'd almost swum out too far. How you'd had to dump the snorkel and mask. It was a close one, you'll tell them. I called out but you didn't hear. No one heard. Best be more careful next time, someone will probably say; even when the water looks calm there are still currents. Just because it's warmer than back home doesn't mean you can treat it like a swimming pool, they'll say, and you'll laugh and say, well, I know that now. And everyone will go quiet for a moment, thinking about it, until the waiter comes past and you order another round of drinks. And raise a silent toast to all the good things. The cold wet glass against the back of your sunburnt neck. The trace of her fingers, the soft wet bite of her lips. The juice of an orange spilling down your chin. Music, and dancing, and voices colliding in the warm night air.

You swim, and you rest. It won't take long now. It's not too far. You look up, past the headland and into the next bay along, and you swim and you rest a little more. Sometimes it happens like this.

Supplementary Notes To The Testimony Of Appellants B & E

Bassingham, Haddington

i. Bassingham is a small village situated on the eastern bank of the River Witham, upstream from the major population centre of Lincoln. Agriculture was the major economic activity in the area, along with a range of small businesses associated with the sector: repair-yards, feed merchants, packing-houses and the like. The agriculture was predominantly arable, with a range of cereal, salad and root crops; there was also, prior to the period in question, a sizeable dairy and beef industry in the area, with cattle grazing mainly taking place on the low-lying fields along the river valleys. The population of Bassingham, when last surveyed, stood at 700, although the figure is probably now lower. There are two public houses, a church, and a bridge which carried the road towards Thurlby and Witham St Hughs. The rebuilding of the bridge is nearing completion at the time of writing. There are currently no official school buildings. During the period in question, with formal education suspended due to security concerns, the majority of children in the area were engaged in assisting older family members with the movement and management of livestock, in addition to more informal occupations such as swimming, ball-sports, courtship rituals and evacuation drills.

147

ii. Not proven.

iii. Haddington is a small hamlet of residential and agricultural buildings, situated approximately 300 metres north of the River Witham and a mile south of the ancient Roman road to Lincoln, known as the Fosse Way, which is now a major highway. Satellite imagery suggests that the walk from Haddington to Bassingham would take approximately 45 minutes, via either the Thurlby Road or Bridge Road bridges. It would also be possible, and within the stated context significantly safer, either to cross by the weir at the end of Mill Lane or to ford the river at one of its narrower points and make one's way to Bassingham's outskirts through the low-lying fields in which, reportedly, the crops sometimes grew to above head-height.

iv. The veracity of a claim such as this is not within this report's remit. It is sufficient to observe that, in common with many similar accounts, this section of the transcript serves to demonstrate that the appellants perceived a high enough level of risk for their covert evacuation to be organised by older members of the community.

v. The nearest government military installation to Bassingham/Haddington is at RAF Waddington, six miles to the east; this equates to approximately 90 minutes' walk, or 30 seconds' flight time. Squadrons based at RAF Waddington are predominantly surveillance-oriented; the nearest ground-attack aircraft are based instead at RAF Coningsby, which is a further twenty-one miles – or 60 seconds' flight time – to the east. Aircraft based here include the Eurofighter Typhoon, which carries the Paveway IV laser-guided bomb system (using a modified Mk-82 general-purpose bomb with increased penetrative abilities and an optional air-burst fusing system) as well as the Mauser BK-27 revolver cannon and AGM-65 Maverick, AGM-88 HARM, Storm Shadow and Brimstone air-to-surface missiles.

vi. Satellite imagery does in fact indicate that between Haddington and the river lie the remains of what is believed to be a former manor or grange, with a series of raised earthworks, ditches, ponds and a former medieval dovecote providing few clues as to the original form or function of the building, or to the identity of its once wealthy inhabitants. There is however no current evidence to support these claims of recent excavation, or burial.

vii. Understood to be a reference to the Prince William of Gloucester (PWOG) barracks, located on high ground to the east of Grantham, overlooking both the town and all major north–south routes. The base, while also serving as a logistics and training centre, is home to five squadrons of government army reservists known as the 'Territorial Army'. These are soldiers not ordinarily resident within the barracks, but rather spread widely across the region, embedded in civilian positions and not uniformed until such time as their services are required. They are available to be called into service at very short notice, and can move to active patrol readiness within a matter of hours.

viii. Unconfirmed.

ix. Due to their ages at the time, and the lack of independent verification from the period in question, the exact route taken by the appellants and their associates/guardians is impossible to verify. But it can be noted here that a walking route directly south from Bassingham and Haddington would pass close by the PWOG barracks, and in any case through territory where any civilians may have been unidentified 'Territorial Army' personnel. An alternative route is likely therefore to have led through the area around North and South Rauceby, heading towards the fens which run alongside Forty Foot Drain. On this route, visibility could have been clear as far as the coast, and any approach would have been observed from some distance. There are also in this area numerous culverts and ditches which serve to drain the fields, as well as assorted agricultural buildings such as sheds, workshops and barns, any of which may have been suitable as hiding places or places of shelter or refuge.

x. This chronology is supported by an extract from the testimony of Appellant F, in section 24.5 of transcript 72: *'I was worried about it, yeah. Of course. I knew we weren't going to be back for like a long time. My mum was all worried because I was so young, and she was scared of what might happen on the way, and plus it was such a long way. Yeah, so. She asked me not to go. But everyone else was going, so we all got like up for it and that and we went. This was November that year like. I was eleven, yeah? We were just walking, yeah?'*

xi. This appears to refer to a route taken through the areas formerly known as Cambridgeshire, Bedfordshire, Hertfordshire and Essex. The route is unlikely to have been direct, being influenced by local militia movements during the period in question as well as by the uncertain motives and navigational abilities of the appellants' guardians. The landscape along this route is for the most part of gently undulating farmland, dotted with quiet villages and isolated settlements and intersected by a network of river and canal systems. The relatively level terrain would have enabled the appellants and their associates to cover larger distances than might otherwise have been expected, depending on the security conditions and the available diet.

xii. It may be pertinent here to reproduce an instructional leaflet which was apparently in wide circulation during the period in question [Archival Reference LNS-2029-ff-201.01]: *'Careful preparations should be made before setting out. Appropriate clothing should be worn, including proper stout and waterproof boots. Clothing necessary to keeping warm and dry should be worn or carried. Dressing in layers is recommended. Sun-cream and a sun-hat should be carried, as well as waterproof jacket and trousers. [...] Take a small first-aid kit, and know how to use it: incidents may occur many miles from the nearest house or village, and even five miles can be a long way to walk with a broken ankle, shattered pelvis, or projectile wound. Never travel alone [...], even for short periods of time. Take care when lighting fires. Always boil drinking water. Keep out of watercourses or flooded areas wherever possible. Note local information on landmine placement and other UXO or IED hazard, where such information can be trusted. [...] Be very wary of strangers. Take careful note of weather forecasts and changing security conditions and be prepared to alter your plans accordingly. Never tell anyone where you are going. [...]'*

xiii. Some notes on landmines and other explosive devices follow, and may serve to illustrate this particular section of Appellant B's testimony (which remains unverified, if compelling). With acknowledgments to the Explosive Hazards Advisory Group. Landmines are a cheap and effective weapon which can be deployed across large areas by relatively untrained combatants. Whilst the injuries caused by landmines are often, by design, not immediately fatal, they can lead to death unless rapid medical assistance is provided. Injuries typically include the severing or partial severing of limbs, evisceration, concussion, and severe loss of blood. Unless the victim is evacuated to an established medical centre, wounds sustained in the field will be vulnerable to infection. Some types of mine will be immediately fatal; these include those targeted at vehicles, as well as the 'bounding' type of mine designed to propel itself upwards before detonating its main explosive charge at a height of around three to five feet (i.e. waist- or chest-height). It should be noted that the strategic impact of landmines, and of Improvised Explosive Devices, is as much psychological as it is material; the loss of morale can be substantial, and the impact on the local civilian population is usually significant. Unauthorised movement of goods and personnel, and unwarranted refugee movements, can thus be easily prevented. When looking for landmines, visual clues can include ground colour distortion, depressions in the ground surface, variations in vegetation growth patterns, disturbed topsoil or even protruding elements of the device itself. A tactical understanding of the mine deployment can also provide clues. However, no path or area should be considered safe until it has been systematically checked, cleared, and declared as such.

xiv. See also the public testimonies collected in the publication, *Some of the Boys Didn't Make It* [Committee for the Support of Returnees, Edinburgh Free Press, Edinburgh].

xv. Historically, the depopulated areas of eastern Essex were celebrated for their attraction to the leisure rambler and wildlife enthusiast; reference is made in published guidebooks from shortly before the period in question to *'an ancient landscape of windblown salt-marshes, home to many thousands of over-wintering birds as well as a variety of vegetation such as bee orchid, yellow-wort, southern marsh orchid, sea buckthorn, teasel and trefoil, where footpaths wind along flood-defence banks, passing concrete pillboxes with rusting gun emplacements and an entrancing view of the coast.'* Although it has been noted that during the period in question this area would have seen a population increase as a result of displacement from the urban centres, the appellants' claims in this section of the transcript do appear feasible and thus are considered valid for the purposes of appeal.

xvi. Verified. Note this reference, from the same guidebook referred to in FN xv: *'Remember to bring your binoculars. Remember, also, that while this landscape can be evocative and memorable, it can also be disorientating, with many of the smaller paths and creeks not being marked on the map and tidal flows dramatically changing the topography within the space of a few hours.'* While the associates and guardians travelling with Appellants B and E would have been familiar with wetlands and tidal flows as a result of their geographical origins, it is indeed likely that groups moving through the area from other parts of the country may well have made navigational errors, with results as described in this section of the testimony.

xvii. See also the testimony of Appellant F, section 27.3 of transcript 72: *'Yeah but actually they wouldn't let us go and help. It was too dangerous and that. They told us we had to keep going.'*

xviii. Much of this traffic was conducted not by political sympathisers but simply by economic opportunists, mainly drawn from a local population of fishing crews and ferrymen whose economic activity had been curtailed by the security situation. The boats were often not suited to cross-Channel passage, being typically overloaded and not stocked with life-jackets, food rations or other emergency supplies; passengers were expected to bring any supplies they deemed necessary for the voyage. It is not known how many boats failed to complete the voyages, which were usually conducted by night, but the testimony here does imply that the proportion of failures was known or believed to be high.

xix. Disputed by Prisoner J

xx. This section redacted at the request of the relevant security services.

xxi. The following notes are drawn from an International Red Cross report referring to the period in question, and also from an account published in the *Observer* newspaper, with acknowledgments. The refugee centre on the outskirts of Sangatte, northern France, was based around a large warehouse building originally used by the builders of the now-defunct Channel Tunnel. Upwards of 1,600 people were housed there, in an International Red Cross operation which attracted much controversy. (It is perhaps worth noting in passing that the centre was itself a successor to an earlier incarnation, many years prior to the period in question, which served to house the mainly African refugees and economic migrants attempting to gain entry to the UK.) The refugees slept in tents erected inside the warehouse, with newcomers or those for whom there simply wasn't room sleeping on the concrete floor in the spaces between the tents. Toilet and washing facilities were rudimentary, and often in a poor state of repair. Food rations, usually consisting of bread, soup and hot drinks, were served each day. The refugees were free to come and go, and often made the long walk along a busy road into the town, looking for work, or to make phone calls, or simply for something to do. The refugees tended to organise themselves into groups by nationality, and as their residence became longer-term tensions naturally arose between the different groups. Periodically, the centre was closed down or heavily restricted by the authorities, resulting in large numbers of refugees retreating to the woodland which lay along the high ground overlooking the coast.

xxii. Disputed by Prisoner J, in trial evidence which was ruled proven following sealed submission made by Control Order Subject 00345/B. [Archival Reference HC/7825/P34.03.87; viewing by application only.]

xxiii. This section of the testimony, referring to the forced clearance of all northern refugee sites by French militias believed to have been funded by rogue elements within the French government, is well supported by numerous documentary sources both contemporaneous and retrospective. [See, primarily, vols 2–5 of *The Displacement Testimonies*, De Waarheids Uitgeverij, The Hague: a well-annotated collection of eyewitness accounts and official memoranda, in Dutch and English.]

xxiv. See also testimony of Appellant F, section 32.4 of transcript 72: *'Yeah, they came with guns, with tanks, they killed loads of people, [...] some people.'*

xxv. See also testimony of Appellant F, section 32.6 of transcript 72: *'And loads of people were like abducted, captured yeah? I don't know what happened to them, I don't know what happened to them even now like.'*

xxvi. See also testimony of Appellant F, section 32.9 of transcript 72: *'The ones who could swim, they swam like. They weren't even [...] there was an attack [...] everyone got in and loads of people, they like I guess they drowned or something, they couldn't swim yeah? It weren't even that far to the boats, it was just like a few hundred metres or something. But I knew how to swim from when I was a kid [...]'*

xxvii. This section redacted at the request of the relevant security services.

xxviii. This section redacted at the request of the relevant security services.

xxix. The appellants' chronology is inconsistent with the historical record here, although it should be noted that such confusion on the part of returning refugees is not unusual. It appears likely that the appellants spent a period of eight or nine years (following the five years in the area of Sangatte) in a series of displaced persons camps in the Netherlands. Their return to the former UK appears to have been prompted by the Dutch government's declaration that the draft peace agreement was in force and that displaced persons would no longer be supported within the territory of the Netherlands. It is likely that the appellants' return was via one of the cargo ships which was utilised for mass repatriation at this time, disembarking at Tilbury (which was held, under the terms of the draft peace agreement, by opposition groups).

xxx. The following extract from a widely circulated public information sheet on internal travel, archived during the later stages of the period in question, may serve to illuminate this section of the appellants' testimony: *'When declaring a lift-share request, choose a spot where approaching vehicles have both sufficient time to see you and sufficient space to stop safely. Consider routes leading away from the roadside in the event of possible threat. Make eye contact with passing drivers, but maintain a neutral expression. Be patient. Once a lift has been offered, briefly discuss your destination and that of the driver's while assessing the condition of the vehicle and state of the driver and other occupants. Whilst in the vehicle, make light conversation as prompted by the driver, taking care to avoid politics, religion or the recent security situation. Familiarise yourself with the door and window mechanisms adjacent to your seat; if the central locking has been activated you may still be able to effect an exit using the window.'*

xxxi. This section redacted at the request of the relevant security services.

xxxii. This seems likely. Assuming the appellants' lift-share arrangement left them deposited at the Newark/Winthorpe junction, Bassingham would have been approximately ten miles distant, well within the scope of a day's walk if taking a route via Stapleford Wood and Norton Disney. However, given the changes in the local landscape (felled trees, demolished or partly destroyed buildings, new and significantly enlarged watercourses, earthworks, embankments, etc) which would have taken place during the fourteen years of the appellants' absence, the complex access-rights situation, and the expansion of military bases in the area, the appellants' claim that this journey took three days is presumed valid for the purposes of this appeal.

xxxiii. Reference to the military training area which spreads north from the A17 along both banks of the River Witham.

xxxiv. Aerial surveillance records have confirmed that on this date there was in fact a house on the northern outskirts of Bassingham to which banners and ribbons had been fastened and in which an irregular number of persons had gathered. Haddington, of course, was not habitable at this time.

xxxv. Note that in common with many appellants and their dependants, a confusion has arisen here between military personnel and host officers from the security services. Records confirm that interception in this case was carried out by the latter.

xxxvi. This section redacted at the request of the relevant security services.

xxxvii. The appellants appear unaware at this point that further appeal against the secure relocation process has been refused.

xxxviii. This section redacted at the request of the relevant security services.

xxxix. This section redacted at the request of the relevant security services.

xl. Disputed by Prisoner J.

Thoughtful

Newark

She threw her pint glass across the garden and told him to just shut up. She threw the ashtray as well. Bloody just shut up, she told him. He looked at her. He didn't say anything. He moved his drink away from her side of the table. She stood up and went to fetch the pint glass and the ashtray, tucking them both under her arm while she plucked the cigarette-ends from the damp grass and collected them in the palm of her hand.

She was thoughtful like that.

The Singing

Thurlby

She lay very still, trying not to let the sound of the singing slip away. It was so vivid, and yet so distant. This kept
happening. She could never make out the words, if there
were any, nor even quite a tune. She wasn't sure, really,
whether it could properly be called singing. The sound
was almost beyond hearing, but it seemed to bear some
relation to falling drops of water, or to something molten.
Something whispered, or filled with breath. She thought
it was probably beautiful, and she missed it as soon as it
was gone. This was what happened. She lay very still. She
listened. She could hear her own breathing. The sound of
the hot water in the central-heating pipes. The rush of passing vehicles on the road. A tractor in the fields. Nothing that
sounded like a song. It was gone already. It would bother
her now for the rest of the day, she knew. Her chest ached
from the effort of holding it still. Her eyes felt as though
they'd been weighed shut, pressed down with balls of cold

dough and pennies. She tried to move her fingers. They felt rigid. She heard her breath like a whisper. She felt her blood moving thickly through her.

She had expected days like this, to begin with. That would seem to be the way things were. But she hadn't expected these days to continue for as long as they had, or to come so often and with such weight. She had thought she would find a way to accommodate this. But instead it had only seemed to grow.

She stood at the window. The light outside was thin. The cars on the road came one at a time, with great spaces between them, moving too quickly, and the sounds they left behind were like smears. The light seemed to tremble in the distance, towards the horizon, where the day had already begun. She could see dust rising behind a line of tractors, where they were ploughing in the stubble. She could see birds heading out towards the sea. She thought she could see flames from a burning barn or haystack, but she couldn't be sure.

She turned back into the room. It was quiet. There were so many things to be done, and no one now to do them for.

Wires

Messingham

It was a sugar-beet, presumably, since that was a sugar-beet lorry in front of her and this thing turning in the air at something like sixty miles an hour had just fallen off it. It looked like a giant turnip, and was covered in mud, and basically looked more or less like whatever she would have imagined a sugar-beet to look like if she'd given it any thought before now. Which she didn't think she had. It was totally filthy. They didn't make sugar out of that, did they? What did they do, grind it? Cook it?

Regardless, whatever, it was coming straight for her.

Meaning this was, what, one of those time-slows-down moments or something. Her life was presumably going to start flashing in front of her eyes right about now. She wondered why she hadn't screamed or anything. 'Oh' seemed to be about as much as she'd managed. But in the time it had taken to say 'Oh' she'd apparently had the time to make a list of all the things she was having the time to think about, like, ie *Item One*, how she'd said 'Oh' without any panic or fear, and did that mean she was repressed or just calm or collected or what; *Item Two*, what would Marcus say when he found out, would he try and find someone to blame, such as herself for driving too close or even for driving on her own at all, or such as the lorry driver for overloading the lorry, or such as her, again, for not having joined the union like he'd told her to, like anyone was in a union these days, especially anyone with a part-time job who was still at uni and not actually all that bothered about pension rights or legal representation; *Item Three*, but she couldn't possibly be thinking all this in the time it was taking for the sugarbeet to turn in the air and crash through the windscreen, if that's what it was going to do, and what then, meaning this must be like a neural-pathway illusion or something; *Item Four*, actually Marcus did go on sometimes, he did reckon himself, and how come she thought things like that about him so often, maybe she was being unfair, because they were good together, people had told her they were good together, but basically she was confused and she didn't know where she stood; *Item Five*, a witty and deadpan way of mentioning this on her status update would be something like, Emily Wilkinson is sweet enough already thanks without a sugarbeet in the face, although actually she wouldn't be able to put that, if that's what was actually going to happen, thinking about it logically; *Item Six*, although did she really even know what a neural pathway was, or was it just something she'd heard someone else talk about and decided to start saying?

Item Seven was just, basically, wtf.

*   *   *

Meanwhile: before she had time to do anything useful, like eg swerve or brake or duck or throw her arms up in front of her face, the sugar-beet smashed through the windscreen and thumped into the passenger seat beside her. There was a roar of cold air. And now she swerved, only now, once there was no need and it just made things more dangerous, into the middle lane and back again into the slow lane. It was totally instinctive, and totally useless, and basically made her think of her great-grandad saying God help us if there's a war on. She saw other people looking at her, or she thought she did, all shocked faces and big mouths; a woman pulling at her boyfriend's arm and pointing, a man swearing and reaching for his phone, another man in a blue van waving her over to the hard shoulder. But she might have imagined this, or invented it afterwards. Marcus was always saying that people didn't look at her as much as she thought they did. She never knew whether he meant this to reassure her or if he was saying she reckoned herself too much.

Anyway. Point being. Status update: Emily Wilkinson is still alive.

She pulled over to the hard shoulder and came to a stop. The blue van pulled over in front of her. She put her hazard lights on and listened to the clicking sound they made. When she looked up the people in the passing cars already had no idea what had happened. The drama was over. The traffic was back to full speed, the lorry was already miles down the road. She wondered if she was supposed to start crying. She didn't feel like crying.

*   *   *

Someone was standing next to the car. 'Bloody hell,' he said. He peered in at her through the hole in the windscreen. He looked like a mechanic or a breakdown man or something. He was wearing a waxed jacket with rips in the elbows, and jeans. He looked tired; his eyes were puffy and dark and his breathing was heavy. He rested his hand on the bonnet and leaned in closer. 'Bloody *hell*,' he said again, raising his voice against the traffic; 'you all right, love?' She smiled, and nodded, and shrugged, which was weird, which meant was she for some reason apologising for his concern? '*Bloody* hell,' he said for a third time. 'You could have been killed.'

Thanks. Great. This was, what, news?

She looked down at the sugar-beet, which was sitting on a heap of glass on the passenger seat beside her. The bits of glass were small and lumpy, like gravel. She noticed more bits of glass on the floor, and the dashboard, and spread across her lap. She noticed that her left arm was scratched, and that she was still holding on to the steering wheel, and that maybe she wasn't breathing quite as much as she should have been, although that happened whenever she thought about her breathing, it going wrong like that, too deep or too shallow or too quick, although that wasn't just her though, surely, it was one of those well-known paradoxes, like a Buddhist thing or something. Total mindlessness. Mindfulness. Just breathe.

'The police are on their way,' someone else said. She looked up and saw another man, a younger man in a sweatshirt and jeans, holding up a silver phone. 'I just called the police,' he said. 'They're on their way.' He seemed pleased to have a phone with him, the way he was holding it, like this was his first one or something. Which there was no way. His jeans had grass-stains on the knees, and his boots were thick with mud.

'You called them, did you?' the older man asked. The younger man nodded, and put his phone in his pocket, and looked at her. She sat there, waiting for the two of them to catch up. Like: yes, a sugar-beet had come through the windscreen; no, she wasn't hurt; yes, this other guy did phone the police. Any further questions? I can email you the notes? The younger man looked through the hole in the windscreen, and at the windscreen itself, and whistled. Actually whistled: this long descending note like the sound-effect of a rock falling towards someone's head in an old film. What was that?

'You all right?' he asked her. 'You cut or anything? You in shock?' She shook her head. Not that she knew how she would know she was in shock. She was pretty sure one of the symptoms of being in shock would be not thinking you were in shock. Like with hypothermia, when you take off your clothes and roll around laughing in the snow. She'd read that somewhere. He looked at the sugar-beet and whistled again. 'I mean,' he said, and now she didn't know if he was talking to her or to the other man; 'that could've been fatal, couldn't it?' The other man nodded and said something in agreement. They both looked at her again. 'You could have been killed,' the younger man said. It was good of him to clarify that for her. She wondered what she was supposed to say. They looked as if they were waiting for her to ask something, to ask for help in some way.

164

'Well. Thanks for stopping,' she said. They could probably go now, really, if they'd called the police. There was no need to wait. She thought she probably wanted them to go now.

'Oh no, it's nothing, don't be daft,' the older man said.

'Couldn't just leave you like that, could we?' the younger man said. He looked at her arm. 'You're bleeding,' he said. 'Look.' He pointed to the scratches on her arm, and she looked down at herself. She could see the blood, but she couldn't feel anything. There wasn't much of it. It could be someone else's, couldn't it? But there wasn't anyone else. It must be hers. But she couldn't feel anything. She looked back at the younger man.

'It's fine,' she said. 'It's nothing. Really. Thanks.'

'No, it might be though,' he said, 'it might get infected. You have to be careful with things like that. There's a first-aid box in the van. Hang on.' He turned and walked back to the van, a blue Transit with the name and number of a landscape gardening company painted across the back, and a little cartoon gardener with a speech bubble saying no job was too small. The doors were tied shut with a length of orange rope. The number-plate was splattered with mud, but it looked like a K-reg. K450 something, although she wasn't sure if that was 0 the number or O the letter. The older man turned and smiled at her, while they were waiting, and she supposed that was him trying to be reassuring but to be honest it looked a bit weird. Although he probably couldn't help it. He probably had some kind of condition. Like a degenerative eye condition, maybe? And then on top of that, which would be painful enough, he had to put up with people like her thinking he looked creepy when he was just trying to be nice. She smiled back; she didn't want him thinking she'd been thinking all that about him looking creepy or weird.

'Police will be here in a minute,' he said. She nodded. 'Lorry must have been overloaded,' he said. 'Driver's probably none the wiser even now.'

'No,' she said, glancing down at the sugar-beet again. 'I suppose not.' The younger man came back, waving a green plastic first-aid box at her. He looked just as pleased as when he'd held up the phone. She wondered if he was on some sort of special supported apprenticeship or something, if he was a little bit learning-challenged, and then she thought it was probably discriminatory of her to have even thought that and she tried to get the thought out of her mind. Only you can't get thoughts out of your mind just by trying; that was another one of those Buddhist things. She should just concentrate on not thinking about her breathing instead, she thought. Just, total mindlessness. Mindfulness. Just breathe.

He passed the first-aid box through the hole in the windscreen. His hands were stained with oil and mud, and as they touched hers they felt heavy and awkward. She put the box in her lap and opened it. She wondered what he wanted her to do. 'I don't know,' he said. 'I just thought. Has it got antiseptic cream in there?' She rummaged through the bandages and wipes and creams and scissors. And now what. She took out a wipe, dabbed at her arm, and closed the box. She handed it back to him, holding the bloody wipe in one hand.

'Thanks,' she said. 'I think I'll be okay now.' Was she talking too slowly? Patronising him? Or was she making reasonable allowances for his learning-challenges? But he might not even be that. She was over-complicating the situation, probably. Which was another thing Marcus said to her sometimes, that she did that. She looked at him. He shrugged.

'Well, yeah,' he said. 'If you're sure. I just thought, you know.'

Status update: Emily Wilkinson regrets not having signed up for breakdown insurance.

'Thanks,' she said.

She'd chosen Hull because she'd thought it would sound interesting to say she was going to a provincial university. Or more exactly because she thought it would make her sound interesting to even say 'provincial university', which she didn't think anyone had said since about 1987 or some other time way before she was born. She wasn't even exactly sure what provincial meant. Was it just anywhere not-London? That seemed pretty sweeping. That was where most people lived. Maybe it meant anywhere that wasn't London or Oxford or Cambridge, and that was still pretty sweeping. Whatever, people didn't seem to say it any more, which was why she'd been looking forward to saying it. Only it turned out that no one knew what she was talking about and they mostly thought she was saying provisional, which totally wasn't the same thing at all.

Anyway, though, that hadn't been the only reason she'd chosen Hull. Another reason was it was a long way from home. As in definitely too far to visit. Plus when she went on the open day she'd loved the way the river smelt of the sea, and obviously the bridge, which looked like something from a film, and also the silence you hit when you got to the edge of the town, and the way it didn't take long to get to the edge of town. And of course she'd liked the Larkin thing, except again it didn't seem like too many people were bothered about that. Or knew about it. Or knew how much it meant, if they did know about it. When she first got there she kept putting 'Emily Wilkinson is a bit chilly and smells of fish' on her status updates, but no one got the reference so she gave it up. Plus it made her look weird, obviously, even after she'd explained it in the comments.

She'd met Marcus in her second year, when he'd taught a module on 'The Literature of Marginal(ised) Places'. Which she'd enjoyed enough to actually go to at least half of the lectures rather than just download the notes. He had a way of explaining things like he properly wanted you to understand, instead of just wanting to show off or get through the class as quick as he could. There was something sort of generous about the way he talked, in class, and the way he listened to the students. Plus he was what it was difficult to think of a better word for than totally buff, and also had what she couldn't be more articulate than call a lovely mouth, and basically made her spend quite a lot of time not actively addressing the issues of appropriation inherent in a culturally privileged form such as literary fiction taking exclusion and marginality as its subject. Her friend Jenny had said she couldn't see it at all, as in the buffness and the lovely mouth rather than the inherent appropriation, but that had only made her think it was maybe something more along the lines of a genuine connection thing and not just some kind of stereotypical type of crush; and Jenny did at least agree that no way did it count as inappropriate if it was just a PhD student and not an actual lecturer. His last seminar had been on the Tasmanian novel, which it turned out there were quite a few of, and afterwards he'd kept her talking until the others had left and said were there any issues she wanted to discuss and actually did she want to go for a drink. To which her response had been, and that took you so long why?

There hadn't really been anyone before Marcus. Not since coming to university, anyway. There'd been a few things at parties, and she'd slept with one of her house-mates a bunch of times, but nothing serious enough to make her change her relationship setting. With Marcus it had been different, almost immediately. He'd asked her out, like formally, and they'd had late-night conversations about their relationship and what relationships meant and even whether or not they were in love and how they would know and whether love could ever be defined without reference to the other. She didn't really know. She thought being in love probably didn't mean telling your girlfriend what she could wear when you went to the pub together, or asking her not to talk to certain people, or telling her she was the reason you couldn't finish your thesis.

They hadn't moved in together, but almost as soon as they'd started going out their possessions had begun drifting from one house to the other until it felt like they were just living together in two places. Sometimes when she woke up it took her a moment to remember which house she was in. It wasn't always a nice feeling. Which meant, what? She fully had no idea what it meant. Because she liked Marcus, she liked him a lot. She liked the conversations they had, which were smart and complicated and went on for hours. And she liked the way he looked at her when he wanted to do the things she'd been thinking about in class when she should have been thinking about discourses of liminality, when she'd been imagining saying he was welcome to cross her threshold any day. There was still all that. But there were other things. Things that made her uncomfortable, uncertain, things she was pretty sure weren't part of how a relationship was supposed to make you feel happy or good about yourself or whatever it was a relationship was supposed to make you feel.

She should be calling him now, and she wasn't. He'd want her to have called, when he heard. Something like this. He should be the first person she thought of calling. He'd think it was odd that she hadn't. He'd be hurt. She thought about calling Jenny instead, to tell her what had happened, or her supervisor, to tell her she'd be late getting back to the office. She should call someone, probably, but she couldn't really imagine having the words to explain it and she couldn't face having anyone else tell her she could have been killed and plus anyway she was totally fine, wasn't she? She looked down at the sugar-beet again. Was that what that smell was? It wasn't a sugary smell at all. It was more like an earthy smell, like wet earth, like something rotting in the earth. She didn't see how they could get from that to a bowl of white sugar on a café table, or even to that sort of wet, boozy smell you got when you drove past the refinery, coming up the A1. Which come to think of it was probably where the lorry would have been heading. It would be, what, an hour's drive from here? Maybe she should go there and give them back their sugar-beet, tell them what had happened. Complain, maybe.

The passenger door opened, and the older man leaned in towards her.

'You need to get out,' he said. It seemed a bit too directive, the way he said it. She didn't move. 'It's not safe, being on the hard shoulder like this,' he added. 'We should all be behind the barrier.' They'd been discussing this, had they? It looked like they'd been discussing something. The older man was already holding out his hand to help her across the passenger seat. She looked at the traffic, roaring and weaving and hurtling past, and she remembered hearing about incidents where people had been struck and killed on the hard shoulder, when they were changing a tyre, or going for a piss, or just stopping to help. She remembered her cousin once telling her about a school minibus which had driven into the back of a Highways Maintenance truck and burst into flames. Which meant they were right about this, did it, probably? She swung her feet over into the passenger's side, took the man's hand, and squeezed out on to the tarmac. It was an awkward manoeuvre, and she didn't think she'd completed it with much elegance or style. The younger man was already standing behind the barrier, and she clambered over to join him. She didn't do that very gracefully either. He started climbing up the embankment.

'Just in case,' he said, looking back at her. Meaning what, she wondered. 'Something could flip, couldn't it?' he said, and he did something with his hands which was presumably supposed to look like a vehicle striking a barrier and somersaulting across it. The older man caught her eye, and nodded, and she followed them both up the embankment, through the litter and the long grass.

It was much colder at the top. Sort of exposed. The wind was whipping away the sound of the traffic, making her feel further from the road than they really were. The two men looked awkward, as though maybe they were uncomfortable about the time this whole situation was taking. The younger man made the whistling noise again. She could barely hear it against the wind.

'You're lucky,' he said, nodding down towards her car. 'I mean, you know. You're lucky we stopped. You could have been killed.' She didn't know what to say to this. She nodded, and folded her arms against the cold. The older man arched his back, rubbing at his neck with both hands.

'They'll be here soon,' he said, and she nodded again, looking around.

Behind them, the ground sloped away towards a small woodland of what she thought might be hawthorn or rowan trees or something like that. The ones with the red berries. There were ragged strips of bin-liners and carrier-bags hanging from the branches, flapping in the wind. Past the trees, there was a warehouse, and an access road, and she noticed that the streetlights along the access road were coming on already. Beyond the access road, a few miles further away, there were some houses which she wasn't sure if they were some estate on the outskirts of Hull or some other town altogether. Hull was further than that, she was pretty sure. It was the other side of the estuary, and they were still south of the river. Almost certainly.

The older man started down the slope, towards the trees. 'I'm just going to, you know,' he said. 'While we're waiting.' She turned away, looking back at the road. She was getting colder now. She looked at her car, and at the blue van. They were both rocking gently in the slipstream of the passing traffic, their hazard lights blinking in sequence. She wondered if she felt like crying yet. She didn't think so. It still didn't seem like the right moment.

She would talk to Marcus at the weekend, she decided. He'd understand, when it came down to it. Once he gave her a chance to explain. She'd say something like although they'd been good together at times and she was still very fond of him she just couldn't see where things were going for them. She didn't like the way he made her feel about herself, sometimes. She needed some time to find out who she was and what she needed from a relationship. Something like that.

She'd tried it out with Jenny. Jenny had said it sounded about right. Jenny had said she thought Marcus was reasonable and would probably take it on board, although obviously he'd still be disappointed. That was how she talked sometimes, like she was a personal guidance counsellor or something, or an older and wiser cousin. Whereas in fact she was only like a year older, and had spent that year mostly in Thailand and Australia, which was her version of travelling the world and which she thought made her the total source of wisdom when in fact it made her the total source of knowing about youth hostels and full-moon parties and not even having heard of Philip fucking Larkin. And she was wrong about Marcus. It was way more likely he would shout at her when she told him. Or break something. It wouldn't be the first time. Everyone thought he was so reasonable. But she wasn't going to back down this time. She was certain of it, suddenly. Something like this, it made you think about things, about your priorities. She could say that to him, in fact. She could explain what had happened and that it had made her rethink a few things. Maybe she should call him now in fact, and tell him what had happened. So he'd already have the context when she talked about wanting to finish things. Maybe that would be sensible. She should do that. She wanted to do that, she realised. She wanted to hear his voice, and to know that he knew she was okay. Which meant what. She wanted him to know where she was. Her phone was still in her bag, in the car. She started to move down the embankment. The younger man grabbed her arm.

'You should stay up here,' he said. 'It's safer.' She looked at him, and at his hand on her arm. 'They'll be here in a minute,' he said.

'I just need to get my phone,' she said. 'I need to call someone. I'll be careful, thanks.' She tried to step away, but he held her back. 'Excuse me?' she said.

'You're probably in shock,' he said. 'You should be careful. Maybe you should sit down.'

'I'm okay, actually, thanks? I don't want to sit down?' She spoke clearly, looking him in the eye, raising her voice above the wind and the traffic. Plus raising her voice against maybe he was a bit deaf, as well as the learning-challenged thing. She wanted him to let go of her arm. She tried to pull away again, but his grip was too tight. She looked at him, like: what are you doing? He shook his head. He said something else, but she couldn't hear him. She didn't know if the wind had picked up or what was going on. He looked confused, as if he couldn't remember what he was supposed to be saying.

She glanced down the other side of the embankment, and saw the older man at the edge of the woodland. He was standing with his back to the trees, looking up at the two of them, his hands held tensely by his sides. What was he. He seemed to be trying to say something to the younger man. He seemed to be waiting for something. She tried to pull away. But what.

What Happened to Mr Davison

Cadwell

First of all I want to start by saying we all of us just really have every sympathy as regards what happened to Mr Davidson. Obviously the conclusion was not one which I or any of us were seeking. That goes without saying. I mean, I honestly don't think that what happened was within the range of foreseeable consequences. Not that we sat down and undertook a full risk assessment before embarking on that particular course of action. Of course not. It was more of a spontaneous, spur-of-the-moment type of scenario. But I think even given how little forward analysis was involved it would be safe to say that the outcome was not one any of us envisaged. I mean, clearly not. That's just not the kind of people we are, any of us. I think that's just really understood. I think I'm safe in saying that that's been accepted, by some of the people who've been impacted upon, in terms of the subsequent turn of events. Including Mr Davidson himself. As far as we've been able to gather.

I mean, you know, some of the people he has around him have been understandably cautious, in terms of what I suppose you could call access. That's been my understanding at least, to date: that an approach of that manner would not be favourably received at this time, given the ongoing circumstances. I'm speaking in terms of with reference to third parties, in this context. Given our feeling that a direct approach would be likely to have been deemed insensitive, in light of the wider context, and the history and suchlike.

Davison. Yes. Of course.

Right.

I'm not sure there's actually any need to rehearse the facts of the day in question. I think everyone's very familiar with the sequence of what went on. Suffice it to say that the context was rather a pressured one. Myself and the other three gentlemen in question have discussed this at length, and we all agree that any of the precursors to our actions would in and of themselves have been sufficient as to be considered intolerable; but it was the combination of those precursors which led to the rather hastily agreed-upon course of action which was then taken.

Yes, I would concede that it was hastily agreed-upon.

No, I wouldn't support that notion. That doesn't necessarily follow.

I can't recall which one of us specifically initiated the proposal. We've spoken about this as well, and we are all in agreement that the proposal arose as a more or less spontaneous initiative between us. We take collective responsibility on that point. Which is to say, on the limited point of how and by whom the proposal was initiated; that was a collective responsibility, I'm saying. I'm not talking about the wider question of responsibility for the eventual outcome. Not at all. That's very much a matter for debate. I think we can all agree on that. And of course that's a debate I would welcome, when the time comes. No one would welcome that more than me. But my feeling is that this wouldn't be the appropriate context for that discussion, not today. My understanding was that this was simply an opportunity to clarify the narrative, as it were.

Thank you. Yes. I will.

Yes, quite so. The background. So. Mr Davidson and myself have been near-neighbours for a number of years, understanding of course that neighbour is a relative term in that neck of the woods. His house is visible from our house, and his land abuts on to ours. I wouldn't say that we've become close friends over that duration; he's a busy man, understandably, and although I spend as much time in that property as is possible I wouldn't class myself as a full-time resident, by any means. So our opportunities for interaction have been naturally limited. But there hadn't been any animosity between ourselves. Not historically speaking.

I wouldn't say surprised as such, no. One expects a certain amount of countryside activity in the countryside, clearly. Possibly the range and duration and volume of those activities did somewhat exceed our expectations, yes. But we understood that our grounds for complaint were fairly restricted. Mr Davidson was a farming man, after all, and that much was perfectly clear at the time we purchased the property, and indeed Mr Davidson was absolutely entitled to reiterate this fact from time to time, as he felt it necessary to so do.

Davison. I stand corrected.

Quite, absolutely.

Well, it's just that I would dispute whether motorcycle scramble racing can be considered to be a farming activity. Harvesting is one thing, even allowing for the fact that at times it went on until two or three o'clock in the morning. Constructing a new intensive poultry-production unit is also one thing; notwithstanding one's own personal views on the merits of such a farming method, it is still classifiably a farming activity. But motorcycle scramble racing is just quite another thing altogether, I'm sure we can agree. I mean, look, I understand the need for economic diversification as much as the next man, especially in this day and age. I really do. I just wonder whether there's such a thing as being too diverse.

Oh, I'd hardly know where to begin. It wasn't just the noise, although that was of a peculiarly piercing and high-pitched quality which I have to tell you was just about consistently unbearable. But noise is one thing. No, it was more the fumes, and the dust, and the type of people it brought to the area. I mean, the dust was unbelievable. The situation was extremely unpleasant, at best.

Intolerable was a word I used earlier, you're quite right. I stand by that.

Oh, now hang on. By saying type of people I simply meant to refer to the behaviour in terms of road-use, parking on verges and blocking driveways and bringing in large vehicles which the road there simply isn't designed to be capable of coping with. I didn't mean to cast aspersions. Far from it. This whole thing had nothing whatsoever to do with that. It wasn't the late-night music we objected to, nor the type of language we sometimes heard being used in the designated camping area which happened to be in the field adjacent to our garden. No. This was simply a question of the dust, and the fumes, and the overall intrusion into and disturbance of our lives.

Yes. That is my understanding of the prognosis.

Quite.

Well, yes, of course I would agree that Mr Davidson's life has now been disturbed, absolutely. But I think that's rather an emotive way of framing the situation, if you don't mind my saying so. The outcome of our actions on that day cannot in any way reflect upon the reasons we felt we had for taking those actions. Look, the situation had been recurring for months. And on this occasion, with guests at the house who were able to see the situation anew and emphasise to myself just how utterly unacceptable it was; well, the phrase I recall being used was this will not stand. You know, this simply will not stand. A line needed to be drawn. I had guests in my home, and I was effectively being humiliated by the situation. And so that was the background to the decision which was taken by myself and the other three gentlemen in question.

Possibly it was an emotive decision, yes. I do accept that.

Yes. Yes I do. I do believe it was a proportional response. Clearly the eventual outcome of the resulting chain of events was tragically disproportionate. But our original actions were reasonable, I feel, under the circumstances which I've gone to some lengths to outline for you today. And look, you know, the criminal proceedings relating to the earth-moving equipment, and the taking without consent thereof, have been concluded to the satisfaction of the Crown Prosecution

Service. So that matter is actually now closed, I believe.

Right. I understand. Indeed.

Well, look, you know, regret is a very difficult word. It's a complicated word. Do I, in all hindsight, wish things had turned out very differently? Of course I do. We all do, fervently. Would I have undertaken an alternative course of action had what we now know to have been the outcome been clear to me at that time? Absolutely I would. But the fact remains, the outcome wasn't at all clear to any of us at that moment in time. As I've said, we were operating very much on a spur-of-the-moment basis. Something had to be done. The situation was intolerable. Of course I regret what eventually came to be seen as the outcome of the chain of events which the four of us perhaps somewhat inadvertently set in motion. But I'm just not sure I can accept the premise that this means I should regret my actions at that particular juncture, or the very limited decision-making process which led to those actions. Would an expression of regret change one single iota of the outcome of that day, or the impact upon Mr Davidson and his family? Of course not. Would such an expression somehow absolve myself of the burden of responsibility which I so rightly bear upon my own shoulders? Quite frankly, I fail to see why it should.

Look, of course I feel a sense of sadness about what happened to Mr Davidson. Of course I do. But this apprehension that somehow we should all go around apologising left, right and centre for a whole host of actions which clearly we are completely powerless to go back and rectify; well, I just don't buy it. I absolutely don't. None of us do.

Davison. Right. Of course.

Years Of This, Now

Grantham

She sat beside the bed and watched him breathe. She pulled her chair closer, the metal legs scraping across the floor. She'd been here barely ten minutes, and already she wanted to leave.

She should be praying now, she supposed. But she didn't know what she would be praying for, if she were to pray honestly; whether she would be praying for his healing or simply asking not to have to be here at all.

The machines beside his bed did what they needed to do. His chest rose and fell.

She tried to remember when she'd last prayed for anybody. The thought of it seemed almost ridiculous, now. She reached out and held his hand. It was warm. She held it between her two hands, and she thought she felt some small pressure in response. Was that possible? She closed her eyes. She opened her eyes and looked around. The door to the main part of the ward was open, but nobody was watching. She could hear the nurses talking in their little side-room, further down the corridor. She could hear a television beside one of the beds in the ward. She turned back to Michael, and closed her eyes. Keep him safe, she said, silently. It was all she could think to say. Keep him safe and well. Keep him on this road to recovery. Or, no; keep him.

She opened her eyes, shocked at herself.

She leaned forward and smoothed the hair away from his forehead. It was getting long again. And he needed a shave. She wondered whether the nurses would do that. She pulled the sheet a little higher up his chest. She watched his breathing, his stillness. It was a long time since she'd seen him as relaxed as this. Even his sleep had seemed restless and tense of late; his arms wrapped round himself, his jaw clamped shut, his fists clenched. The doctor had warned him, in a way; if not of this exactly then of something. You're too busy, the doctor had said, too stressed. You're in need of a break, in need of some exercise, in need of a better diet. In need, also, of being able to pay attention when someone who knew what they were talking about said something like that, rather than thinking he was too young or too strong or just too bloody blessed for it to apply to him.

No, that wasn't fair. Michael had paid attention, but he'd had no idea what to do with the information. I can't have a break, he'd insisted. How can I have a break? How would the parish go on without me, at a time like this? There wasn't a time when it hadn't been a time like this.

She wondered whether it was a male trait, this notion of being trapped by one's own indispensability, or if it was something exclusive to Michael.

She shouldn't be angry. It wasn't fair. He was dedicated to his job. That was a good thing. The world needed people who were dedicated to their jobs. That church needed a vicar who was dedicated to the parish, finally. But she was tired of it now. She was tired of being left alone while he did these things. This new parish was supposed to have been a chance for them both to take things a little more slowly. It was supposed to have been a refreshing change after the urban pressures of the last parish; a nice quiet country church to see them both into retirement. Long walks. Coffee mornings. Ladies seeing to the flowers. The occasional trip into the city to go to the gallery, the cinema, the restaurants.

Whereas instead he'd managed to find a country parish which had years of problems stacked up, where the church had to be kept locked and the congregation was unwilling to lift a finger and all the hard-luck stories from miles around still managed to find their way to the vicarage door.

She pictured him being alone when it had happened, laid out on the vestry's cold stone floor. He'd managed to reach his mobile phone, it seemed, with one side of his body numbed into sudden immobility and a terrible fear clouding his brain, and when he'd fumbled for the redial button her work number had been the first to come up. It was the secretary in her department office who'd called the ambulance. I could hardly hear him, she told Catherine afterwards. It wasn't even a whisper.

And *stroke* was such a strange word for someone to have given this thing. It was misleading, underhand. Not that she could see much of the violence which had been done to him. There was nothing of the awful drooping grim ace she'd seen on others who'd suffered strokes. Perhaps that would come later. For now, he just looked rested. As handsome as ever, in fact. He'd always been a handsome man, his looks seeming only to deepen with age instead of sagging and softening the way hers had done. She had been beautiful once, she thought – he'd told her often enough that she'd believed him, eventually – but that was mostly gone now, her figure rounded, her hair dulled, her skin marked and lined by the years. It felt as though their pairing had grown more uneven over the years, not less. And now there was this.

Because there would be years of this, now. If she stayed. His frailty, his dependence, his doing the things the doctors had told him not to and then looking to her to stop him. Everyone looking to her. People asking her gently how he was, when he would be back at work, whether he was thinking about early retirement. Adding *And how are you?* only as an occasional afterthought.

She heard the low hum and squeak of a floor-polishing machine moving along the corridor. Whoever was watching the television in the main ward turned it up a little to compensate. Somebody leaned through the doorway, apologised, and disappeared. The machines beside Michael's bed did what they needed to do. His chest rose and fell.

She tried to imagine being somewhere else. Being contacted after the fact by his sister, or a doctor, or even by some other woman. Having to decide whether to visit. Having that choice. She found it impossible to actually picture not being here with him. To picture being with someone else when, as would surely happen again, the telephone call came. Somebody saying, *It's Michael.* Somebody passing on the news of Michael being in a hospital bed once more, with wires taped to his chest and an oxygen mask across his face. She wondered how that would work, when it came to it. Whether this someone else would give her a lift to the hospital, whether they would wait downstairs or come up with her, whether there would be some residual awkwardness, still, or only concern, affection, love. Would they all be friends, in fact? Is that how these things worked? Would they have, what was it called, *moved on*?

The someone else was the hardest part to imagine. Some other woman. Some other man. It seemed impossible, now.

And what was all this in aid of, anyway. Where was she going with all this. She should just be praying for him to get better. Instead of all this speculation. All this might be and could be. Why was she even allowing herself? Hers wasn't the sort of life where choices presented themselves, and held equal weight, and remained dangling within reach. Other people had these lives, it appeared. Other people were able to choose not to live with regret.

* * *

This would be the most selfish thing she had done, by far. She wasn't sure, now, whether she would be able to go through with it. But it didn't need to be anything she was going through with, really. Not initially. She was just going on a retreat. It had been booked for months. Nobody would think badly of her for going. Michael might not even know.

Michael might not know anything again.

She wondered how long his sister would take to get here, and whether Michael would be awake by then. She imagined his sister reading the letter she was going to send once she got there; what her reaction would be, what she would tell Michael. She wondered whether she and her husband would move into the vicarage for a time, or whether they'd persuade Michael to move in with them.

She wondered whether anyone would forgive her for this, whether they would understand. She doubted it. But doubt no longer seemed like a good enough reason for not doing something.

The machines did what they needed to do. His chest rose, and fell.

She tucked his hands back under the sheet and stood up to leave, putting on her coat and picking up her suitcase and pouring him a glass of water from the jug on the bedside locker, in case he was thirsty when he woke up.

The Remains

Friskney

Are believed to still be intact. Are understood to be within an area of approximately seventeen square miles. Are believed to have been concealed. Are either partially or completely buried. Are likely to be without clothes or jewellery or other possessions. May not be suitable for visual identification. Will be treated as a critical evidential scene. Have been the subject of much intrusive and unhelpful press speculation. Continue to be a key focus of questioning. Will be located using a combination of aerial surveillance and ground-penetrating radar. May be beautifully preserved, tanned and creased and oiled, by the action of the rich peated ground. May be laid in a resting position with legs together and hands folded and head turned gently to one side. Are of course still a concern to everyone in the department. May be intact. Have continued to be a topic of periodic speculation from time to time over the years. May be

crammed into a box or bag or case. May need to be identified by recourse to dental records. May be wholly or
partially lost due to action by animal or animals. May
be wrapped in a silken winding sheet and buried with
jewellery and other possessions pressed neatly into the
folded hands. Must be in a location known to person
or persons as yet unidentified. Could well be recoverable given the relinquishing of certain key details
known to person or persons unknown. May have been
visited from time to time by the perpetrator or individuals known to the perpetrator. Are either partial or
complete. May ultimately need to be recovered using
a team from the forensic archaeology department. Are
not currently a priority in this challenging period of
strained resources. Have yet to be found. Continue to
be the subject of an open case file. Have yet to be found.
Have yet to be found. Have yet to be found. Have been
destroyed by water. Have yet to be found. Have yet to
be found. Have yet to be found. Have yet to be found.
Have yet to be found. Have yet to be found. Have yet to
be found. Have yet to be found. Have been destroyed
by earth. Have yet to be found. Have yet to be found.
Will not give you what you need. Have yet to be found.
Have yet to be found. Have yet to be found. Have yet
to be found. Have no further purpose to serve. Have
yet to be found. Have yet to be found. Have yet to be
found. Have yet to be found. Have been destroyed by
fire. Have yet to be found. Have yet to be found. Have
yet to be found. Have yet to be found. Have yet to be
found. Have yet to be found. Have yet to be found.

Have yet to be found. Have yet to be found. Have yet to be found. Have yet to be found. Have yet to be found. Have yet to be found. Have yet to be found. Have yet to be found. Have yet to be found. Have yet to be found. Have yet to be found. Will not bring her back. Have yet to be found. Have gone. Have yet to be found. Have yet to be found. Have yet to be found. Have yet to be found. Have yet to be found. Have yet to be found. Have yet to be found. Have yet to be found. Have yet to be found. Have yet to be found. Are gone. Have yet to be found. Have yet to be found. Have yet to be found. Have yet to be found. Have yet to be found. Have yet to be found. Is gone. Have yet to be found. Have yet to be found. Have yet to be found. Have yet to be found. Have yet to be found. Have yet to be found. Have yet to be found. Have yet to be found. Have yet to be found. Have yet to be found. Are gone. Have yet to be found. Have yet to be found. Have yet to be found. Have yet to be found. Have yet to be found. Is gone. Have yet to be found. Have yet to be found. Have yet to be found. Have yet to be found. Have yet to be found. Have yet to be found. Have yet to be found. Have yet to be found. Have yet to be found. Have yet to be found. Have yet to be found. Have yet to be.

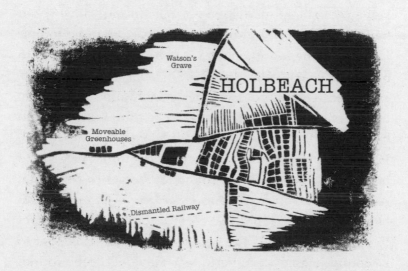

The Cleaning

Holbeach

He had no idea where to begin. So much had been ruined.
He stood in the hallway and felt the carpet sinking wetly
beneath his boots. The smell was rising, already. She peered
in from the front path, her arms folded, saying she didn't
even think she wanted to come in. He waited. What did she
know. She had no idea.

'There's nothing in there, is there? What if something's
got in?'

Of course there was nothing in there. The building had
been checked and secured. But she wouldn't come in until
he'd looked. So he turned away from the door and walked
through the hall into the kitchen, the playroom, the lounge.
He went upstairs, keeping close to the wall as they'd been
warned to, and into the bathroom and each of the bedrooms
in turn. He stood at the window of the children's bedroom,
at the back. The other gardens were piled high with rotten
carpets and sofas and beds. It was weeks since the waters

had finally receded. It felt strange to be looking out on solid ground. He remembered the last time he'd been here, holed up with the children, waiting for the boats to come, trying to make a game of it. He looked at one of the girl's paintings, tacked to the wall. She'd painted it a few days before the storms had come. It showed the three of them eating their dinner, him and the girl and the boy. It was spotted with mould and curled almost in half. It would have to go. All these things would have to go. He walked through to the front bedroom and looked down at her. She was stepping from foot to foot, her hands clasped together. He opened the window, and she looked up, sharply.

'Is it okay? Is it clear? Should I come in?'

He told her it was fine. He told her to come in. She had no idea. She hadn't even been there. She thought she knew what it had been like, but really she didn't. The children hadn't told her anything. She hadn't asked. She just thought she knew. He came down the stairs just as she stepped into the hallway. Her hand went up to her face, to cover the smell. Her feet sank into the sodden carpet. Somewhere around the top of her head, a thick black smear marked where the water had risen to. Above it, the wallpaper's stripes looked almost fresh. Below it, they were blurred and streaked with mud.

'It'll be okay though, won't it? We can get this all cleaned up. We'll be all right, won't we?'

She didn't seem to know what she was talking about. She wasn't even looking. Everything was ruined. Everything was completely and totally ruined. The carpets and the floorboards would have to come out. The plaster would have to be knocked off the walls, the wiring redone. It would take months. It would be easier to walk away. Just like she had done. He still didn't know why she'd come back. He didn't know what she wanted from him now, from any of them. He wondered if it was the going away she felt bad about, or just the timing of it. He wondered if she realised how much the children associated her going away with what had happened. He watched her rubbing at the wall, and looking at the muck which came away on her fingers. She sniffed at it. Bloody hell. What was she doing. She took a picture down from the wall, wiped the glass clear to look at it, and threw it out on the front lawn. He went out to the car to get some tools and some gloves. He looked at the picture. When he came back into the house she was standing in the lounge, holding up one end of the rotten sofa, waiting for him to take the other end. She had no idea.

The Last Ditch

Kexby

<u>Notes for discussion points to be raised at next house-meeting, re: early preparation measures needing to be actioned asap:</u>^{endnote i}

Perimeter:
Existing drainage ditches already form natural boundary. Enlarge these to create realistically defendable space.[1] Use spoil to create raised bank behind. Plant raised bank with 3 rows hedging:

– outer row, thorned (blackthorn, hawthorn etc)
– middle row, dense (box, yew etc)
– inner row, fruit-bearing (sloe, rosehip, hazel, raspberry, blackberry, etc)

---

1 Aerial photographs of site are available from departmental archives, cross-referenced to SRN 0010-5586. Note that the notion of a 'realistically defendable space' is, at best, a relative one.

Benefits: wind-shelter for crops within site, visual barrier, physical obstruction. Last point most vital: ditch <u>must</u> be wide enough to prevent vehicles approaching, & hedging <u>must</u> be dense enough to prevent penetration.[2]

Research poss. extra line of defence within hedging perimeter (spiked poles, tripwires, traps etc) to be erected at short notice in emergency.

Above creates obvious vulnerability at entry/exit point. Suggest moveable barricade to be wheeled into place when req. (Booby-trapped?) NB vulnerable entry/exit can be advantage; provides expected focus for attack/ defence.

Successfully defended space as detailed above carries risk of entrapping occupants in siege situation. Plan tunnel construction to enable final escape from poss. prolonged siege. Tunnel to originate in cellar of main house and surface prob. in ▬▬▬▬ woods. Approx 450 metres, forced ventilation req[3].[ii]

Reject options such as eg electrical fencing, floodlighting, automatic gates & barriers, etc; defence options <u>must</u> be resilient to loss of power.

Reject also watchtowers, etc; would attract attention both currently and at time of crisis. Suggest planting

---

2 At time of writing, this ditch and hedging project is at very early stages. It's difficult to see the group achieving the stated depth/width while restricting themselves to the use of handtools, and with the limited labour on site. The proposed hedging would, I have been advised, take approx 10–15 years to reach the desired maturity.

3 Tunnel project likely to pose risk to participants: the stated 'expertise' appears limited to much shorter and shallower excavations. Recommend preventative measures, to include legal steps if necessary. Risk to less-willing members of group would appear to be unreasonable.

fast-growing evergreen at corners of property, to be used as concealed look-out points.

J█████, T████, S████, R████, B██[4] to form Perimeter Working Group. J█████ to then take lead on tunnel. T███ to plan hedge planting & source stock/cuttings. (Tunnel likely to cause most disagreement at group meeting; 'too much time/ work for unlikely purpose' (!) etc etc. Discuss with J█████ before raising at meeting, gain support. Refer to likely results re: children in event of being unable to escape siege. J█████ identifies v. closely with children so this angle likely to be effective.)

Food Production:[iii]

Already well established but dependent on imported supplements. Missing elements inc: cooking oil, sugar, salt, herbs/spices, flour, nuts, staples eg pasta/rice, pulses, other soya-substitute products. Plans for resolving shortfall, to be put to Food Production Group:

– Cooking oil; production would be land-intensive/time-intensive, therefore suggest doing without.
– Sugar; M█████ already researching use of sugar-beet w/ v. mixed results. Likely to be land-intensive. Will recommend extra stores, plus consider alts e.g. honey from beehives? (Controversial, see below.)
– Salt; stores. Trading <u>might</u> be feasible once crisis matures, but in early stages reliance on stores only option. Suggest

---

4 Names and locations have been redacted throughout this recovered document in order to protect ongoing operation. – MK.

acclimatising to significantly reduced usage now. (Propose w/ appeal to health lobby, esp. N██████.)

– Herbs/spices; some already in production. Balance high demand for land against use of herbs/spices in reducing demand for salt, also maintaining appetite.

– Flour; land-intensive & energy-intensive to produce, also energy-intensive to use (baking bread, cakes etc). Recommend other staples in place (primarily potato, also poss. oats). Concede to including some flour in stores; purchase chapatti flour 'in error' as this then has dual-purpose & could be transferred to PWG[5] if required.

– Nuts; include in planting plans.

– Staples; pasta & rice unviable. Switch to potato as main staple.

– Pulses; increase production of runner beans/peas, harvest and dry for stores.

– Soya products; M██████ has already researched soya-milk production, with good results (altho taste an issue). Recommend production of soya, as important source of protein. Also not attractive to raiders, could be used at point of greatest visibility as deterrent/decoy.

Other food production well in hand; fruit trees, fruit bushes, vegetable beds, potato beds, salads etc in polytunnels. Transfer 'leisure' sections of site to food production, eg lawn, children's play area, wild flowers etc. (Children req. to work at time of crisis anyway.)

---

5 Perimeter Working Group. Presumably refers to use of fine flour in Improvised Explosive Device. Subject not known to have training or expertise in preparation or use of explosives. – MK.

Concern over visibility of food production; address this with reference to PWG. Note risk of aerial surveillance, altho obv. reduced risk of this at time of crisis.[6]

Obv. gap in food-production plans = animals. Chickens for eggs & meat, bees for honey, poss. pigs for meat; wd be low-input in terms of time/land/feed requirements and high-output in terms of protein (& pig meat v. storable, ditto honey). BUT v. unlikely to be passed by group as currently constituted; majority opposed to animal use, despite apparent awareness of risk posed by coming crisis. Possible negotiating strategies to include:

– advocate bee-keeping 'only' for pollination purposes, later to suggest non-harmful harvesting of 'small' amount of honey.
– arrange 'rescue' of chickens from other locations, near end of laying period. Ensure cock 'accidentally' included in this group. Advocate using eggs as they appear; also allow number of successful hatchings. Allow natural lifespans/ natural deaths; at later stage, arrange accidental deaths + advocate use of meat.
– ditto 'rescue' of young pigs.
– Alternative to above: gradual reconstitution of group membership to one with more practical approach to coming crisis. (See Group Analysis, below, esp. recommendations re fewer young children/old people.)

---

6 Presumably refers to fuel shortage restricting flights of any kind. Subject seems not to have considered fuel stockpiling by authority. – MK.

Food Reserves:

Stores already being built up; continue & accelerate this process. Note need to include multi-vitamin supplements, emergency feed rations, and medical supplies (see Exit Strategies, below).

Calculate level of stores req. to cover approx 24 months supply, eg equiv. 2 failed/stolen harvest seasons. Develop secure and/ or concealed storage sites within main property. Also consider poss. secondary storage dump (v. well concealed) adj. to exit point of tunnel, to be utilised in event of escape from siege situation. (Need to be minimal, eg 1 x backpack per escapee.)

Energy:

Wood-fuel for heat & cooking. System already in place, but currently reliant on import. Obv. need to a) build up large store in advance of crisis, this store to be v. well hidden & poss. rigged for defence; b) increase planting of coppice wood, eg willow etc, also pollarding of nut trees etc. Also clear need to reduce wood-fuel requirement by eg additional insulation measures, move towards predominantly raw-food diet, reduction in size of group.

Electrical energy generation already being researched and implemented, with R▬ taking lead. Reiterate need for v. low-tech/low-maint. solutions; all parts/skills for repair must be available on site! Bring this up again at next meeting; PV[7] impractical for this reason?

Remember crisis will reduce energy requirements anyway: computers/phones/TV become redundant.

---

7 Photovoltaic, aka 'solar panels'. – MK.

(Non-networked electronic entertainment wd be negotiable.) Main req. wd therefore be lighting: may need to adopt blackout policy anyway, to avoid drawing attention to site or property.

(General note: will need to balance appearance of dereliction & unattractiveness with not actually looking abandoned enough to encourage occupation attempts. This will need to be improvised by reference to local properties. But blackout likely starting point.)

Water/Waste:

Compost toilets already fully functioning. Obv. need to ensure high hygiene standards maintained – any digestive illness wd be disastrous at time of crisis. Recent lapses in hygiene practice have been noted – to raise at next meeting. Need for additional rainwater collection & storage. Cd be most important (& overlooked) aspect of crisis – energy restrictions will wreck mains water system. Also prone to sabotage by vested interest and/or forced medication by authority (eg emergency population reduction?).[8]

Relations with other Groups/Community:

Strong policy trend within group to building greater links with local community and with other s/s[9] groups regionally. Need to argue against this. Risk of spreading resources too thinly, + raising awareness locally of resources here, + risk of exploitation and/or betrayal. (Theft, bad faith,

---

8 Typical misunderstanding of authority plans for Emergency Mass Medication, common among groups of this type.

9 'self-sufficient'. – MK.

attack, occupation, information-passing, etc etc.) Also risk of undue emotional attachment which would impact decision-making at time of crisis.

<u>Group Analysis:</u>[iv]

8 adult members of group (6 male, 2 female), w/ at least one other female + infant attempting to join. One current member not full-time resident, although otherwise fully committed.

3 children (plus potential infant).

Analysis:

J▉▉▉ – late 30s, in relationship w/ R▉▉, 2 children. Good health. Expert in tunnel-digging, also general construction etc. Likely early member of PDTFG.[10] High understanding of likely impact of crisis. Father of D▉▉▉, 10 month old, son of L▉▉ who he had brief relationship with last year. L▉▉ & D▉▉▉ now want to join group; with obv. emotional/dynamic impact.

P▉▉▉▉[11] – late 20s, currently single, 1 child not resident at property w/ minimal contact (good). Very good health. Expert in construction, strategy, logistics, unarmed combat. Early member of PDTFG (obv!). High awareness/understanding of crisis.

T▉▉ – late 50s, divorced, children not known of, minimal contact w/ ex-wife & apparent minimal emotional attachment/concern. Background in forestry/conservation(!), expert in planting & plant maintenance, also expert in

---

10 Primary Defence Task Force Group. – MK.

11 Author of this document. – MK.

insulation/draught-proofing etc. Likely to be unsupportive of PDTFG, or any form of force resistance; but also unlikely to actively oppose it.

S███ – early 50s, 13 y/o daughter, Z██, relationship with Z██'s father unknown & undiscussed. Not always in good health. Unsupportive of crisis strategies; argues in favour of closer ties with local community. Poses significant risk to maintenance of secrecy. Current links w/ wider community risk issues of emotional attachment at the crisis time.

R███ – late 30s, in relationship with J█████, 2 children (T███, 5, B█████, 8). Expert in electrical generation & maintenance. Also likely early member of PDTFG; has mentioned being in Cadet Force while at school, so useful expertise. Good understanding of crisis, altho sceptical (& sarcastic) at times.

B██ – early 20s, v. enthusiastic & energetic altho w/ limited practical skills. Key member of PDTFG, also of PWG. Prime potential for links with weapon sources; altho discussion of these links raises separate concerns & needs to be handled carefully. Good health but drinks & uses drugs v. heavily. Emotional attachments unknown; has alluded to number of short-term relationships within activist & party circles, unclear how these arise or are terminated but no evidence of undue emotional impacts.

M███[12] – early 30s (??), no known relationships or sig. emotional ties. Expert in unarmed combat, also enthusiastic contribution to construction tasks. Well connected in activist circles, thus often absent from site, but contributes

---

12 Reference to this officer. – MK.

well to workload anyway. Apparent ready access to cash & willingness to contribute. Highly engaged in discussion of crisis & response; some members of group critical/ wary of this. Not yet discussed PDTFG, but likely to be keen early member.

N█████ – mid 60s, minimal relationship ties (has alluded to ex-partner & children, but no known contact with them to date; whereabouts unknown). Expert in food production, crop management, storage, etc. Prime source of expertise within group in this field. Often in poor health, w/ tendency to unusual diet & supplement regimes to combat this. Strictly vegan. Also has pronounced pacifist tendencies; has referred to surrender as a viable option in the face of armed assault, has also argued in favour of close links with local community and other resilient groups. Dangerously influential, altho presents as soft-spoken/passive etc etc. Will need to be kept <u>completely</u> unaware of PDTFG.

Children – ages 5, 8, 13. Also possible 10-month-old baby joining group. 13 y/o and 8 y/o should be able to contribute useful labour at time of crisis & in preparation for it. 5 y/o obv. less use & req. more resources (also reduces available labour from parents). Admittance of baby wd be v. poor choice by group: extra resource demand + v. reduced labour from that parent; also significant burden in event of siege/tunnel/escape procedure; also at high risk of ill-health and resultant emotional strain. (Also, parent-age situation in this case will presumably cause sig. probs w/ relationship dynamics, tensions & conflict etc, at cost to effective co-operation and shared labour.)

Re 13 y/o girl, note that presence is useful in terms of long-term breeding reqs. of group.

Group Analysis Summary:
Good mix of skills and experience. Mostly good health. V. young and v. old members of group remain a concern; continue to slant discussions towards options for leaving site and being replaced by members of more appropriate age; when sourcing replacement members suggest addressing current gender imbalance with view to long-term breeding reqs. of group.

Majority of group <u>are</u> engaged w/ problem of crisis & preparation for it, altho small maj. opposed to armed defence. However, small minority not always serious in their discussion of issue; provocative/sarcastic/unhelpful. Recent remarks to effect that sexual activity/attachment wd reduce attention to detail as re crisis preparation were particularly unhelpful. Predict this minority won't always consider subject worthy of humour.

Assessment of External Threats:
Working down from top:
Assume, at crisis, central & local authorities will withdraw to defendable spaces with existing supplies/stocks, & not form any threat to resilient groups across the periphery of their territory.

Police/military will be primarily focused on maintaining order in larger population centres and/or protecting significant infrastructure. (Certainly on protecting any remaining supply chain, eg any food production

& distribution centres which are able to continue functioning.) Threat from police/military therefore likely to be limited: however police/military also unlikely to prevent threats from other parties such as eg:

Immediate neighbours. Early stages of crisis likely to see requests for assistance from local residents, followed by unpleasant coercion/emotional blackmail etc, followed by covert attacks (attempted night-theft) or co-ordinated overt attacks (direct armed assault, eg by mob w/ hand-tools or by pseudo-militia w/ weapons). Covert attacks shd be prevented by perimeter defences & by good surveillance. Overt attacks will need to be repelled by direct display of superior force, deadly force if req. (See Defence, below.) Since a large & co-ordinated overt attack will have a numerical advantage it will be important to prevent one arising. Careful surveillance & intelligence (perhaps by false negotiation) could assist in this; a pre-emptive strike or strikes may become necessary.[13]

Mobile groups. As the crisis matures, mobile groups may well develop, poss. from major population centres; these will be small groups and majority young/male. Likely to be physically weak due to fatigue of travel + unreliable nutrition; but prob. well armed (esp. if from major pop. centres) & experienced/uninhibited in use of deadly force. These groups will be the prime threat as crisis matures: careful surveillance will be essential, as will avoiding unnecessary awareness of site. Research plan for decoy vulnerable site

---

13 Serious cause for concern here. Potentially substantial risk of subject misperceiving environmental factors and moving into 'crisis' mode, with the results clearly detailed here. Recommend continued surveillance of subject. – MK.

(eg lit, smoke from chimney, obvious food supply) which can be booby-trapped.[14] Prepare others in group, esp. members of Primary Defence Task Force Group, for use of deadly/overwhelming force. (Again, utilise reference to poss. impact on children in event of defence failure as motivating tactic.)

Rogue loners. Individuals unlikely to survive crisis, as limited amount of co-operation will be req. However some are likely to appear, esp. in early stages, and will have advantage of low profile. Reminder that sustained & effective surveillance, with appropriate follow-up action, will be essential throughout period of crisis.

Defence:[15]

Refer to notes on perimeter, above. Also camouflage, discretion, etc. These grouped as Passive Defence. Surveillance also part of this.

Need for force is likely to arise however.[v] Training in unarmed combat already in progress among some members of group; bring recommendation that all undertake this training to the next meeting, and that 'unarmed' be gradually redefined to inc. use of sticks, staves, shields, handtools, knives, etc, up to and including deadly force. (May need to be careful about phrasing of this; may need to

---

14 Again, potential use of explosives and/or 'traps' is cause for concern. – MK.

15 Note this entire section with High Concern. Recommend that this section of recovered document be highlighted and forwarded to Command. Plans to obtain this level of hardware – although of limited practicality – would if carried through put this group into a High Risk category. Recommend continuing surveillance, with mobile team assigned. – DC (MK's Supervising Officer).

introduce tools/knives etc at later date. But good training & preparedness is essential asap.)

Use of weaponry will be inevitable in crisis situation: many members of group not yet reconciled to this, and alarmed by talk of it. Need to work discreetly with others (B██, R██, J██) to make progress in obtaining items+ammo, & training. Shotgun, rifle, handguns in first instance. But also need low-tech/low-maintenance solutions; prepare construction & use of crossbows and/or traditional bows. Sourcing weapons will be primary difficulty. B██[16] has referred to connections in major population centre which may be of use – expensive and poss. dangerous, but prob. only option. Of prime concern wd be to avoid alerting sources of weaponry to our existence and/or whereabouts; these wd by definition be groups we'd want to avoid knowing about us in the crisis time.

Ideally, a range of weapons wd be obtained. A silenced sniper-style rifle wd be preferred option; allows for early strike without attracting attention and without risk to operative. Concealed handguns useful for surprise element, eg within a false negotiation situation. Wide blast-radius shotgun useful for close confrontation. Obv. selection will be limited by availability. (It may be a useful precaution to also source 1 or more automatic weapons, to be reserved for defence against a large-scale assault, eg by a mobile group.) (However, note that in this

---

16 Secondary target subject, with pre-assigned Subject Reference Number 0010-5622. Already known. Recommend renewed surveillance with reference to possibility of making contact with known criminal gangs in attempt to source weapons.

situation it may be more prudent to opt for a siege+tunnel strategy.)

Training in the use of these weapons will be almost as difficult as the obtaining of them, particularly while an element of secrecy within the group is required. (Altho clearly an element of secrecy from the wider community will always be required.) Options include trekking to sites such as beaches, woodland, etc. Abandoned quarry or railway tunnel wd be ideal. Further research req.

<u>Exit Strategies:</u>

Above plans notwithstanding, crisis may reach point of severity/duration where managed exit becomes preferred option. Group have so far been unwilling to discuss this when raised, but vital to prepare options on their behalf. (Alts. wd be poss. capture by eg mobile groups, immediate neighbours, active authority figures, etc. Poss. scenarios include but not limited to: forced labour, forced extraction of resource information, rape (female <u>and</u> male), captive human food source, use of violence as local entertainment, etc).

Options inc:

Medical (eg morphine, cyanide, v. large quantity of eg ibuprofen)

Mechanical (hanging in roof space w/ prepared ropes, primed tunnel collapse, primed demolition of property, crushing w/ rocks/timber/metal objects)

Environmental (exposure on high open ground, starvation, self-harm + deliberate wound-infection, weighted entry into watercourse to effect drowning)

Weapons (self-administered gunfire (or co-administered in case of weak/unwilling/young), knives and other tools to effect rapid bleeding, confrontation w/ armed groups in such manner as to effect death by gunfire)

Any proposed method must be a) quick, b) low-pain/distress where possible, c) non-rescindable, d) enforceable/enactable by others if req.[vi]

<u>Notes to Self:</u>

Keep no further records. Discuss only with members of group relevant to completion of specific tasks. Maintain personal morale. Liaise with M███[17] on more controversial aspects; he has similar perspective on chances of crisis, likely impacts & req. steps etc, and has been helpful esp. in group meetings; is also able to listen to detail and discuss wide range of topics without recourse to humour/sarcasm, and is in general terms a v. useful ally!

Destroy these notes.

---

17 Again, reference to this officer. – MK.

[Endnotes follow. General remarks on viability of group and practical outlook for their programme of activities. Comments on individual subject. Recommendations for ongoing strategy (includes collated recommendations from footnotes). – MK]

[i] This document comprises a photographic reproduction of an original document authored by surveillance subject in question (SRN 0010-5586). Photographic record was covertly obtained during conversation with subject; the original document is believed to have now been destroyed.

[ii] Summary of defence measures adopted by group: weak. Perimeter easily breachable by tracked vehicle, and likely to remain so in future. Main entry breachable by non-tracked vehicle in conjunction with minimal necessary force.

[iii] These are all standard policies and procedures for a group of this nature, and pose no risk to wider community. (Withdrawn: non-required personal opinion. – DC, MK's Supervising Officer)

[iv] Subject's assessment of group is reasonably accurate, although it is this officer's observation that he overestimates the engagement of other group members with what he terms 'crisis preparation'. Secondary observation: subject is at times isolated within the group, very preoccupied with the issues and plans documented here, and vulnerable to criticism or light humour being made of this fact. As such, subject has been well-exposed to this officer's approach, and appears to have responded to minor praise and encouragement with a trusting and open outlook towards this officer. This appears likely to continue, especially given little prospect of subject attaining romantic or sexual ties within the group.

[v] See footnotes within main document for response to this section. General observation that while desire to obtain weaponry is genuine and forcefully expressed, this officer retains doubts about viability of plans to do so and limited capacity to utilise any such obtained weaponry. Close surveillance will focus on this issue, however, as instructed by DC.

This emphasis on suicide methods being 'non-rescindable' and 'enforceable by others' is alarming, and raises the prospect, as discussed in Footnote 6, of subject misperceiving a given situation and potentially 'enforcing' one of these methods on other members of the group. Surveillance will need to focus on any steps taken to prepare these methods, and subject may need to be referred for covert psychiatric assessment.

Summary of Recommendations – DC:

- Continued surveillance of subject, with additional resource of mobile surveillance unit as required.
- Renewed surveillance of SRN 0010-5622, focusing on contacts with known criminal gangs and/or attempts to source weaponry and ammunition.
- Periodic aerial reconnaissance.
- Preventative measures regarding proposed tunnel construction: covert dissuasion, covert obstruction, preventative arrest and/or psychiatric treatment.
- Retain covert and/or compulsory psychiatric assessment and treatment as an option in the event of advanced steps being taken to prepare 'enforceable suicide' methods.
- Location to be added to Food Resources Requisition Site List within the revised Emergency Planning Documents.
- Location/group to be added to the Firearms Confiscation Site List, also within the revised Emergency Planning Documents.
- Subject and other members of group to be added to Internment List, also within the revised Emergency Planning Documents.
- Local community to be covertly reinforced as recommended in the Information Strategy section of the revised Emergency Planning Documents; specifically recommend Procedures 22, 27, and 34. ('Scientists are divided on so-called global warming', 'New oil-deposits being discovered every year', and 'Green energy: meeting our nation's energy demands in the coming century', respectively.)

Dig A Hole

Nottingham

A man lies in a field beside a river, flat on his back in the short wet grass. His leg is turned awkwardly beneath him, and his face is bent out of shape with pain. Another man looks down at him and says, angrily, that it's not his fault. Around the four edges of the field, a large group of people, mostly men, are shouting. 'Dig a hole and fucking bury him,' they shout, repeatedly. 'Dig a hole and *fucking* bury him.' There are twenty thousand of them, pointing in his direction and shouting as one. 'Dig a hole and *fucking bury him.*'

The man smiles to himself, in spite of the pain and the thought that he might have broken his leg. He knows they don't mean it, really.

I Remember There Was A Hill

Colcby

There was a hill, and on the hill there was a road. The road was narrow and straight and it went straight up the side of the hill. The road was broken, with ruts, and holes, and streaks of mud where tractors or tracked vehicles must have turned in and out of the fields on either side. The road was lined with poplar trees, and hawthorn hedges, and then as the road flattened out the hedges gave way to stone walls, and brick walls, and the low fences of front gardens, the front gardens of the houses that made up the village that sat like a fortress at the top of the hill. And in that village there was no green nor park nor pub nor church nor school nor shop; only the two dozen houses set back from the road, none of the houses looking out towards the sea but all turned inwards facing the road, the doors all closed and the windows all closed and the curtains all closed and no one tending their roses or mowing their lawns or mending their roofs or painting their window-frames, and no one chasing a ball or walking a dog or passing the time of day or taking a bike from a shed or hanging out laundry or washing a car or getting into a car and driving out on to the road to make their way down the hill. No barking dogs. No hum of distant lawnmower, nor rumble of tractor. No sudden cracking sounds of guns. No music or drums. No marching feet. No posters taped to telegraph poles which told of flower shows or village fêtes or meetings of the neighbourhood watch. No parish noticeboard. No markings on the road, no signs noting entry to the village and asking visitors to drive with care. No signs displaying the village name, nor the year the prize for Best Kept Village was won, nor the name of the village's foreign-sounding twin. There was a phone-box, beside the road, and a phone which had just started to ring.

The phone-box was beside a dry-stone wall. There were sheep on the other side of the wall. The sheep were in a narrow field which fell steeply down the hill, and the grass was still wet with the night, and the ground was pitted with rabbit-holes, and at the end of the field there was a row of poplar trees and a pile of dead wood and around the dead wood there were nettles growing and beyond the trees and the dead wood there was a view of the land running away to the sea. There were no other hills. There was no other high ground. There were trees. There were towers such as church-towers or water-towers or town-hall towers and on all these towers there were windows or ledges or rooftops or viewing platforms of one sort or another. There were no rabbits in the field. The sheep were huddled up against the wall. The sheep were terribly thin. The phone rang. It was clear that these trees would grow tall in the gardens of these houses and beside the road and in the hollows and boundary-lines of the land between the hill and the river and the sea. That they would rot from within and grow heavy-limbed and in some strong wind come crashing down into these houses and across this road and into the ditches down below, and that new trees would grow up in their place. That the grass of these lawns would grow prairie-tall and thorned briars reach up and twine around the houses and break through crumbling window-frames and pull the brick walls down. That these sheep would die, like all the others, and the uncut crops rot in the fields and the dead chaff be blown into the ditches and clog the ditches and the floods sit heavy on the land for seasons at a time and the roads crumble and the way be passable only by tracked vehicles or airborne vehicles or those wary few who might come through on foot.

The phone-box door was heavy but the hinges didn't creak. The windows of the houses set back from the road were still curtained and dark and the curtains didn't move. The ringing of the phone echoed loudly inside the box and the ringing would not stop. The door was opened. The phone was lifted. First: there was a low humming silence. Then: the wet click of a mouth being opened to speak. Then there was a voice which spoke. Two planes came low across the sky in silence towards the sea, and the sound which followed was like the sound of improvised explosive devices in a culvert very close by.

The sheep scattered blindly across the field towards the dead wood beneath the poplar trees. The heavy door of the phone-box banged shut. The sounds all faded away.

217

Song

Grimsby

Chinese restaurants, launderettes, baked-potato vans.
These are a few of my favourite extractor-fans.

I'll Buy You A Shovel

Marshchapel

We'd been sat there all evening listening to the music and the laughter come over across the fields and we'd run out of drink about when the sun went down. Ray kept looking over in the direction of the Stewart place and I knew what he was thinking but I wasn't about to say it for him. The two of us sat there looking into the fire and the pallet-wood kept cracking and spitting and we were waving off midges and all these shrieks of laughter kept coming across the fields.

Fuck it, he says, in the end. Let's go, he says.

I went off and got the car started.

Just let me do the talking, he says.

*

We knew about the set-up they had over there. We'd been watching them bring it in all week. The marquee and the catering tent. The bar. The sound system and the dance-floor. The flowers and balloons and candles and drapes and linens and fancy chairs. Old man Stewart had been keeping himself busy driving around all week, off to town and back and who knows where else. Directing operations, was what he was probably calling it. The roads were hardly big enough for some of the stuff they'd been bringing in. On Thursday a furniture lorry had come past and stopped at the end of the road by the dead-end sign and spent about ten minutes trying to turn round. We sat outside the caravan and watched. Weren't enough room to turn a lorry round. The reversing alarm kept going on and off and the lorry kept edging backwards and forwards, trying to keep out of the ditch. They could probably have heard that reversing alarm as far down as the Sands. Jackie came down from her house to watch. It was a nice day. Hot, but with a bit of a breeze coming in off the sea. I offered Jackie my seat but she said not to bother. She asked how the ditch was going. Ray told her the ditch was going fine and did she want a smoke. Jackie looked up towards the hay meadow at the top end of the site and round at the fishing lake and back down at us and just sort of didn't say anything. She didn't need to. We'd been there the best part of a month and we'd dug about six foot short of fuck-all. Ray did one of his sighs and stood up and told her again it was going fine. He said we were just waiting to get some advice on the soil hydrology and then we'd crack on. She looked at him. He looked at her right back. The reversing alarm from the furniture lorry chimed out across the fields. A Tornado went over and dropped a bomb on the Sands and vanished over the horizon in silence.

Jackie started speaking just as the noise of it caught up so neither of us heard a word she said. She turned and walked back to the house and looked up at the hay meadow again on her way. Waddled is more of the word. Not to put too fine a point on it. She's not what you'd call petite. She holds her weight like that. Ungainly, is a word you could use. We watched her go. I asked Ray what was he talking about soil hydrology, and he said to keep out of it. He went back in the caravan and shut the door and turned the radio on in there. The furniture lorry finally got turned round and came back along the road and stopped. The driver called down to ask if I knew where the Stewart place was and said something about bloody satnav. I climbed up the bank and pointed him back to the end of the road and told him it was down that way. Weren't a dead-end like the sign said, I told him, you can go through the farmyard and out the other side and the Stewart place is the second on the left. The look on his face. Thanks for letting me know, he said. I said not to mention it, and I went off and mucked about with stakes and string until I didn't think Jackie was looking out of the kitchen window of her house on the other side of the lake there any more. Pond is more like the word, with the size of it. But they're not going to get any customers for a fishing pond, so they're calling it a lake. The furniture lorry drove past again and turned left through the farmyard at the end. Another Tornado went over and dropped a bomb on the Sands. The stakes and the string made a pretty nice line coming down from the hay meadow to the edge of the lake. Made it look like the job was near-enough halfway done.

Ray came out of the caravan. We took the short way across the fields to the Stewart place and watched the lorry driver unloading the chairs and tables and linens, and when old man Stewart came out of the house to sign for everything we cleared off back to the caravan again.

The fishing lake was old man Stewart's. The lake and the land around it and the house where Jackie lived and the hay meadow and the three fields between here and the Stewart place. Also the pine plantation between the Stewart place and the Sands. Also possibly the caravan, although not even Jackie was sure about that and anyway it didn't seem like something he'd want to argue over. It had just always been there she'd told us, when we first moved in, and always seemed like about the right word. We were supposedly on-site security and maintenance, was the idea. We were there to provide a presence. Also to undertake certain unspecified maintenance tasks. Such as for the only example so far digging the ditch to provide drainage from the hay meadow into the lake. There wasn't really any money involved, but the situation suited us and I think it suited Jackie as well in terms of some kind of company and not having to be on her own all the time. But she said old man Stewart had started getting on the phone and asking what was he hearing about these new people on the site, meaning Ray and me. Jackie said it was he was unhappy about the progress but it was also probably due to he knew certain things about certain things which had occurred a great many years previous, certain things which Jackie also had a fair idea about but which she appeared to be putting in the category of now we deserved a second chance but which old man Stewart was apparently placing into quite a different category. Some people have very much longer memories than other people, is what it came down to.

The night before the wedding Jackie was sitting outside the caravan and telling us what she knew about the rest of the Stewarts. Most of the family had arrived that afternoon and most of them had needed to ask for directions, shouting something about bloody satnav down from the road and waving their phones around to try and get a signal. The family were all down south now, was what Jackie was telling us. Hadn't been up this way for years. Most of the crowd tomorrow will be from London, she said. That's where the groom's from. They're talking about it'll be near enough two hundred of them there. One of Jackie's cleaning jobs was at the Stewart place, was how come she knew all this. She started off naming names, like who was who in the Stewart clan, the ex-wife and the sons and the half-brothers and the nephews and nieces, but we weren't really listening. I was breaking up another pallet for the fire and Ray was either looking at the stars or else his head was back like that because he was asleep. We could hear most of the Stewarts out the back of their place, shouting and laughing. I asked Jackie how come with all these relations old man Stewart lived on his own and most of them couldn't even find their own way to the house. Ray said something about therein lay the tale. Without lifting up his head. He actually said therein. Me and Jackie just sort of looked at him, and tried not to laugh, and Ray sat up and rolled a smoke without offering one to anyone. Therein. Jackie asked me had I got the pallet from behind the caravan and I told her yes. She said she'd been planning on using those to make the fishing jetties with. She said she'd told us that. Wasn't much I could say to that, with my foot halfway through the pallet and the fire spitting away like it was. I didn't know much about fishing lakes but I thought it would probably take something better than pallets to build the jetties with. I told her well I was sorry about that but I was sure we could get some more. Ray lit his smoke and said we'd definitely get her some more no need to worry about that.

It wasn't like me or Ray knew enough about fishing to build a fishing lake. We were just there to do a few jobs. I'd never been fishing in my life but I could see this pond wasn't up to much. It was full of green algae or something like that. She'd told us it needed cleaning up and some oxygenating plants putting in and we'd nodded like we knew what she was talking about. She'd said she was going to mainly stock it with roach and carp but she wanted it all fixed up first before she placed any orders. I couldn't see how that overgrown drainage ditch was ever going to support a living creature but I kept my mouth shut. Ray had said something about using barley-straw to freshen up the water and she'd looked impressed. Don't know where he got that. Could have picked it up from all the reading he'd done when he was working in the library.

When she said goodnight and set off walking back to her house on the other side of the lake Ray watched her and asked me if I would. I said he was joking I would. He shrugged. He said he might do only it would depend on the situation. He said something about gravity and big women and then he went off in the caravan and shut the door and turned the radio on in there.

I sat there with the moon shining off the water and the bats twatting silently about and the noise of all those Stewarts barking out across the fields like each of them was trying to be the last to stop laughing. The groom was probably sat outside another back door somewhere now, smoking a last cigarette and listening to all that and wondering what he was letting himself in for.

A Tornado went over and dropped a bomb on the Sands. First time they'd done it in the dark that I knew of. I felt the shadow of it first and like the weight of the heat of it, and then the noise came dragging behind like it always did but it seemed much louder in the dark and I covered my head with my arms until it had passed. I heard shrieking from the Stewart place, and men laughing, and I got up and pissed on the back wheel of Ray's car and went to bed.

Ray was a Muslim at one time. He converted when we were inside. You wouldn't have thought it to look at him. He never had the beard or the hat or anything but he took it very seriously. He changed his name to Abdul Wahid and went to the prayer-room five times a day with the other brothers and took down all the graven images from his cell. I asked him what he was going to do with them. He said it wasn't permitted for any man to make images of the human form which Allah has created or something, so I bought them off him for a SIM card and a pack of tobacco. They were pretty fucking graven. I asked him how come he'd turned Muslim all of a sudden and he said he'd heard the voice of Allah calling to him. I asked him was it just like that out of nowhere and he told me it was out of the blue. He'd been up all night doing press-ups and reading a translation of the Koran he'd got hold of from working in the library and he'd been fasting for three days just to see what it was like, but yes basically he had totally out of the blue heard the voice of Allah. Calling him by name, he said. I didn't ask whether the voice had called him Abdul Wahid or Ray. Turns out the voice of Allah didn't have much else to say so he just kept calling whichever name it was. Ray said it was like nothing else he'd ever heard. He said it was like a light going on inside his head. He said it was like being called home. Which I didn't think was something he would have been hankering after particularly but I didn't say as much. Maybe that's not what he meant. He told me the whole experience had left him feeling blessed. He said it about three times and I believed him even though right then we were standing in line waiting to slop out. But you could see it in his face, the way he felt about it. He asked me how I'd be able to resist if I'd heard the voice of Allah calling me home. I told him that's fair enough Ray, and good luck and all that. He said it wasn't Ray it was Abdul Wahid.

I'm not too sure how things worked out with the whole Muslim thing after that. He spent most of his time in the prayer-room or with the other brothers and I didn't really see him. There was word went round that he'd only converted because someone had been rinsing his gravy-boat and the best protection around was getting in with the brothers, but I don't know if that was true or what.

I've never asked him. I got transferred a long while before either of us got out, and we lost touch after that. This was years ago we're talking. And when I saw him again at the start of the summer it seemed like he'd gone back to calling himself Ray. I wasn't sure, but he didn't look like he was feeling too blessed. He certainly weren't forswearing alcohol. Could be he was still a Muslim but he'd toned it down a bit. Could be that was what he was up to when he kept going back in the caravan and turning the radio on in there.

Someone at the Stewart place tested out the sound system first thing on the Saturday morning. Nine am on the dot, like they'd purposely waited for what they thought was a respectable time. Didn't seem like a respectable time to me. Ray near enough punched a hole in the caravan wall. They played a few tunes and then they started talking on the microphone. Seemed like they didn't really know how loud it was or at least how far sound can travel around here. This was some of the younger Stewarts, it seemed like. Old man Stewart was probably already out somewhere, like straightening the cushions on the church pews or something. They said a few things they obviously thought wouldn't carry as far as the church, and then there was a howl of feedback and a noise like the wrong plug being pulled out and it went quiet again. Ray got up and went outside and I heard him pissing against the wheel of his car. He came back and got two cans of Guinness from the bag by the door and asked if I wanted some breakfast.

We sat by the lake and drank the cans and threw stones into the water. We could see a few cars pulled up outside the church already, three fields to the north. Old man Stewart's Range Rover was there. I asked Ray what he thought about the line I'd staked out for the ditch. He said it was the finest line of stakes he'd ever seen but I needn't think he was about to start digging anything at the weekend when we didn't even have the right tools anyway. I threw some more stones into the water. They made holes in the green algae and then the holes closed up. It happened pretty quickly and then it was like nothing had happened. I wasn't sure how Jackie thought she was going to get all that cleared up. A car pulled out from the farmyard at the end of the road and stopped. A woman got out and tied a sign and some balloons to a telegraph pole. We watched her. She got back in the car and drove along the road and stopped at the top of the bank and got out and tied some more balloons to the telegraph pole there. She looked about the right age to be the bride's mother, dressed in presumably her wedding outfit already. We waved but she didn't see us. Ray shouted hello and waved again and she looked down to where we were sitting. Ray asked if the balloons were to help people find their way to the wedding and she said they were. She was wearing a big wedding hat, and holding on to it like there was a wind blowing a gale. Ray told her that was a good idea, that it was easy to get lost round here even with the bloody satnav. She nodded and smiled and got back in the car and drove off. She drove along and stopped and got out and tied balloons to every telegraph pole between us and the church.

The weather was clear and still and already warm. It was a good day for a wedding, if you liked that sort of thing. I finished my Guinness and threw the can with the others in the ditch at the bottom of the bank and went and had a look around the lake. Ray asked was I going for some kind of leisurely stroll and I gave him the finger. I was wondering how many fishing jetties would fit around the lake and how close you'd put them and how you'd get them to float. I was starting to think we might as well get on and do some of the jobs Jackie had talked about. Since we were here anyway. Might be good to feel like we were getting something done. She'd need some more pallets though.

A couple of vans drove past. They looked like they were from the catering company. Ray waved as they passed but I didn't see anyone waving back. He got up and went in the caravan and came out with another couple of cans. Another van came past, from the off-licence in town. We didn't bother waving.

Late in the morning Jackie came down with a couple of plates of fried-egg sandwiches and said if we were going to be having that sort of a day we might as well get a lining in our stomachs. Meaning the drinking, it seemed like. She had this look on her face like she was indulging us. She said but Monday we'd have to get some work done otherwise old man Stewart would want to have words. She said it was still his land at the end of the day. She called him Mr Stewart. We didn't say anything. We ate the sandwiches. The yolks were soft and the whites were crisp round the edges. We both said they were good sandwiches. Jackie kept looking over towards the church. There were more people standing around outside, and balloons tied to the gateposts at the entrance to the field they were using for a car-park. We'd offered to help with that, earlier in the week, either with the rolling out or even with the like traffic control on the day, but old man Stewart had just looked at us like we weren't even there until we'd turned round and left. Jackie was wearing this sort of flowery orange dress and a straw hat and Ray asked her if she'd been invited to the wedding. She said she hadn't, but she might take a wander over there and see how things were going and see what the bride was wearing and see the flowers and everything. A Tornado came over and dropped another bomb on the Sands. Ray finished his sandwich and licked his fingers clean and told Jackie her dress looked nice. She gave him this look like she was waiting for the punchline and then when there wasn't one she didn't know what to say. Another Tornado came over and then something like a dozen or two dozen Tornadoes came over at the same time and dropped bombs on the Sands and we just stared up at them and the sound was like the actual ground being ripped open. Fucking, asunder. We all crouched down without realising and it took a minute or two to straighten up again once they'd gone.

Ray said the wedding would most likely be ruined if they kept that up all day. He looked pretty pleased about it. He said it would have been a major operation to get the whole squadron in the air and formed up like that, it would have taken serious logistical oversight and a fair amount of groin on the part of the pilots. He said he didn't think they'd be doing that for nothing. One of his uncles had worked on the base for a while, in the kitchens, meaning that was another thing Ray liked to sound knowledgeable about to anyone who'd listen, meaning the planes, not the cooking. I tried to say something about it looking pretty serious now, but I couldn't hear anything I was saying. I was still waiting for the rushing noise in my ears to fade away and basically what felt like my internal organs to fall back into their rightful place. I tried saying it again, that it looked like things were getting serious. Jackie didn't say anything. She was just looking over towards the Sands. I remembered the thing about her son. She took our plates back to the house. Ray said it was good of her to wash our crockery as well as doing breakfast. He laughed. I told him to leave it out. I went and got another drink. What was his name. Jackie's son. Mark. Fucksake.

*

I drove to the Stewart place about as slowly as I could. I wasn't feeling overly confident in my driving abilities by that point, plus not in the state of the car either, and plus there could have been people walking back along the road. There weren't any taxis around and that was probably going to come as a surprise to the crowd they had over there. We saw two of them just before we got to the turning, walking in bare feet with their shoes sticking out of their handbags, their arms folded across their chests. They looked young.

That's what I'm talking about, Ray says.

Just the drinks, I say. Nothing else.

Rinse them dishes any day, he says. I thought he was going to make me stop right there, but he didn't say anything else so I carried on and turned in at the entrance to the Stewart place. We passed some older guests getting into their cars and holding on to each other. We drove down a grassed track which led around the back of the house, past some open barns with more cars parked inside. At the far end of the track, just past the turning into the field with the marquee, we saw a girl being sick into a bed of nettles. Her dress was a bit on the short side for her to be bending over like she was. A lad in a pink shirt with a pinstriped waistcoat was stood next to her, holding her hair away from her face and rubbing her back. They both looked over their shoulders at us, squinting into the headlights. The girl had a string of something hanging from her mouth. We could see her knickers. They were black as sin.

That's what I'm fucking talking about, Ray says.

Just the drinks, I say.

*

We knew Mark from school, and for a bit after that. Years back. Spent a bit of time with him. He was all right, he didn't mind getting up to things. Not that there was all that much to get up to. Mostly it was getting hold of some drinks and finding somewhere to go. One time we walked the five miles out to the Sands with a bottle of cider just so we could drink it while we sat and watched the seals. This was the last year of school. Meaning we were fifteen or sixteen. Ray tried chasing one of the seals and ended up turning round and doing most of the running. It's surprising how fast a seal can move, if you start messing around with it in breeding season. That was the day we took a car the first time, when none of us wanted to walk all the way home again. I didn't know Ray knew how to do the thing with the wires, but he said one of his uncles had shown him. We could all drive, just about, but Mark wouldn't take his turn so we kicked him out and made him walk the rest of the way. He never told anyone about it, which was a good start. That was how come we took him on a job soon after, but it turned out he wasn't really up for it. He didn't know what we were doing until we got in through the back door, and then he wouldn't come in any further than the doormat. He kept saying he could hear someone coming, he could hear a car pulling into the yard, he could maybe hear a siren? He was near enough crying by the time we'd finished so we didn't take him on a job again. Ray made sure he knew not to tell anyone.

Could see why Mark signed up, thinking about it. The way he liked things to be done right. He probably liked the discipline of it and everything. Sit tight and wait for orders. It was still a surprise though, him being the fattest kid in the year and everything. No one really saw him after he'd signed up. Besides the other boys in our year who signed up with him. He was off on training exercises and getting rid of all that weight and all that, and then when he was home he probably wasn't meant to associate with us anyway. Must have seemed like a good idea at the time, signing up. He must have thought the worst he'd have to face would be ducking petrol bombs in Belfast or maybe getting rained on for six months in the Falklands. Instead of getting stuck in a broken-down tank in the desert and dying of heatstroke.

Jackie got an earful of all that our-brave-boys stuff after that, all heroic sacrifices and dying-for-all-our-freedom, which if it was me I'd have wanted someone to talk me through how that was supposed to work exactly. Mark sitting tight in that broken-down tank waiting for his orders. Waiting for help to arrive without it ever passing through his big pink head that it was never coming. They gave him a posthumous medal and everything. No wonder Jackie moved out of town. Must have wanted to get away from all that sympathy. Don't know what happened to Mark's dad. He'd been in all the pictures in the paper, I could remember that, the two of them sat in their lounge with their arms round each other, holding up Mark's school photo like some kind of consolation prize. The sofa was hardly big enough for the two of them and all their crying. He must have just gone and done the off.

Fucking heatstroke though. It weren't exactly Andy McNab.

That was all about the time someone did a job on Hilltop Farm, which old man Stewart didn't exactly own but it turned out he had some interest in, and word went round that it was us who'd done it. There wasn't any proof and it got dropped in the end but that didn't stop word going around anyway. That was when most of the trouble started. It was the interest in that job that meant we got caught out, in the end.

Whoever called it Hilltop Farm must have had some sense of humour, round here.

Jackie came over again before she went to the church and told us that if she did get to go to the reception she'd make sure she brought us back some cake. We told her thanks Jackie, that's good of you, we'll look forward to it. Another load of Tornadoes went over, three of them in close formation going extra-low over the Sands without dropping anything. Jackie said that was how they knew last time round that the war was definitely going to start, when they'd started going at the Sands all hours like this. We didn't know what to say so we told her to enjoy the wedding.

By the time we heard the church bells ringing and the guests were all sweeping out of the church and throwing confetti at the happy couple it had been quiet over by the Sands for a couple of hours. Wouldn't put it past old man Stewart to have gone and had words at the base. National emergency crisis or whatever, this was his daughter getting married. We stood up at the top of the rise by the hay meadow and watched them all coming out of the church. Getting into the line-ups for the pictures. Moving apart and coming together and moving apart again and the young lady in the white dress always at the centre. The women all in hats and dresses like at the races. Ray started talking about how women like dressing up for a wedding. Can't argue with that, he was saying. Strappy shoes. High-heeled shoes. Dresses in bold colours and prints. Purple dresses. Red and white floral dresses. Very tight. Above the knee. Figure-hugging, you get me. Dresses they keep tugging at the hemline like they never noticed how short it was when they put it on, you get me. All that hair-dressing. Hats. Summer hats. Summer dresses and summer hats and straps that keep slipping off shoulders. Bare shoulders.

Bare legs. You get me. It was hard to stop him when he got going on something like that. Fucking, monologue is what you'd call it. I asked him could he see Jackie anywhere and he showed me where she was standing off to one side, sort of behind a stone wall. There were a couple of other women from the village with her but she was the only one wearing a hat.

The church bells kept ringing until the married couple got into a car and drove off. That was a lot of bell-ringing. The seals down at the Sands must have thought the end of the world was coming. We watched the whole procession of cars follow the trail of balloons from the church to the Stewart place and then I got another drink and sat by the lake and Ray went and broke up another pallet. It seemed a bit early to be lighting a fire. It was a pretty hot day still.

When he was done he came and sat down and asked if he'd ever told me about the porno he'd written once. I told him I didn't think he had. I told him I wasn't sure I wanted to know. He told me it had been a while ago and to be fair it had just been the once. He picked up some stones and threw them in the lake. He went and got an empty can and set it up on a flat rock by the edge of the lake and came and sat down and said the story had been for his wife. He looked at me. I threw a stone at the can and missed and didn't say anything. I didn't want to know. He told me it wasn't like he'd been in the habit of writing porn but this had been a long train journey and it was just something that had occurred to him to do. He'd thought she might appreciate it. He'd thought it was something he could do for her, while he was away. To surprise her. I said I didn't know he'd been married. He said there were a lot of things I didn't know about him and anyway this was all a while ago now. He told me don't get him started on marriage.

A stone skidded off the ground and hit the can but the can didn't fall and I threw another one. Jackie's car turned into the driveway by her house and stopped. Jackie got out and went into the house and didn't look at us. She wasn't wearing the hat. She must have left it in the car. Ray carried on talking about this story he said he'd written for his wife. It had been really something, apparently. Blindfolds, gasps of surprise, third parties involved, that type of thing. I held up my hand and told him Ray I don't want the details mate. He said fair enough let's just say it was properly filthy. He said he'd really thought she was going to enjoy it, she'd been known to enjoy that type of thing previously, she'd been quite imaginative. You wouldn't have thought it to look at her though, was his next point. He wanted to emphasise that, it turned out. He spent quite a while emphasising that. She was gorgeous, in summary, a lovely woman. Looked like butter wouldn't melt.

There was a whistling noise from the sound system at the Stewart place, and what sounded like microphones being plugged in and out, and then it went quiet again. I went and got another drink. Ray was still telling his story about the porno story. It looked like it was going to take a while. He told me it took him a long time to write it, this story, when he was sitting on this train. He said he kept getting distracted by what he called the old days. I suppose he meant the old days as in when he first met this wife I'd never heard about. He said he hadn't had a clue where the train was going. It was one of those single-carriage jobs and all he could see out the window was fields like this. He said it had been a hot day and all the windows on the train were open and the pages of his notebook kept flapping about in the wind. I asked him when had he ever had a notebook and he said shut up this was a while ago.

They must have started doing the speeches at the Stewart place. We couldn't hear most of what they were saying but the place kept going off in applause and what sounded like people banging their cutlery on the tables.

Ray was still going on about the train, and about how there'd been hardly anyone else on board, just this bloke who looked like a fitter, and a couple of old ladies, and then this girl who was either a young-looking university student or an old-looking schoolgirl, it was hard to tell, she kept staring out the window, she must have had something on her mind, and as it happened she was quite pretty but he was trying not to look because he properly couldn't tell how old she was and you can't be too careful and anyway he was just trying to concentrate on writing this story for his wife because he thought it was something he could do for her, it seemed important at the time, he thought she'd like it, he thought it would help.

I said, Jesus, Ray, don't forget to breathe.

We threw some more stones at the can.

He told me some more about what had been in this story, stuff about firm smacks on the behind and tying hands and stuffing underwear into mouths, that type of thing. I told him I could probably definitely do without the details. They turned the volume up at the Stewart place and we heard someone doing a toast to the happy couple and then the whole crowd of them going *to the happy couple* again. Ray turned and looked in that direction. We were both thinking about the drink they'd be getting through over there. Ray knocked the can over and went and set it up again and we both moved our chairs a bit further back and threw some more stones. He still hadn't finished. He started talking about how self-conscious it had made him to be writing all that stuff down on a train and how he'd had to keep stopping to sort of catch his breath but he wanted to persevere with it because he really thought his wife was going to like it. I said it was making me self-conscious just having to listen to him go on about it and he told me to shut up again. He said they'd got into that type of thing before, on the phone, when he'd been working away from home, and then he got into how all the working away from home might have been part of the problem, all those nights away and the unpredictability of it was how a lot of the arguments had started. I asked him like, what, you had an actual job and everything? He said sometimes it was like he couldn't say the right thing to make it up to her. I asked him if he'd been a travelling salesman or what. He said some days it seemed like she didn't even want him to try, like she wanted him to just turn round and go out on another job. I said I still didn't know if we were talking about actual jobs here. He said it got to the point where he didn't feel welcome in his own house and all he'd ever wanted was a home where he was welcome. I don't think he was listening to me. It was turning out there was still plenty I didn't know about Ray. He kept mentioning things as if I knew about them when really I had no idea. Like the wife thing. Or like a while before when he'd mentioned living in Scandinavia. Or even like was he or wasn't he a Muslim any more or what.

Another thing I didn't know was whether Ray's mum still lived round in town or if she was still alive or what. I didn't know if he knew. Maybe Ray hadn't said anything about it because he was assuming I'd be as much of a cunt about it as he'd been when I told him about my mum. Who I happened to know had passed on, even though it had been a while before anyone had thought to tell me about it. I missed the funeral when I was inside. That was bad enough but it would have been good to know it was going on. This was what I don't know why I bothered telling Ray one night, when we'd first got here and Jackie had told us all about what she wanted doing, and given us some binbags for cleaning out the caravan, and come down from the house with a couple of fresh pillows and said I don't know about the rest of what's in there but if you're anything like me you'll at least want decent pillows.

They wouldn't have let me go to the funeral anyway but it would have been nice to have been told. It was up in Scotland. Scotland of all places. She never would have wanted to be buried there. She only went up there because her bloke said he'd had enough of it round here and he was going back to Scotland whether she wanted to go with him or not. She told me that, the last time she visited before she went up there. She was good at visiting, I'll give her that. Given everything that had gone off. She said I could go up and join them when I got out, if I liked. While I got back on my feet. Right, I said. Scotland. She said would I write, and I said yes I would, I'd write. I'd definitely write. What was she thinking, Scotland. She must have hated it up there. She never would have wanted to be buried there. I knew she wouldn't. That was what I told Ray about. Scotland had more or less come up in conversation somehow, so that was what I told him about. I said she should have been buried down here, where her family were buried, where the rest of her family still lived. People could go and visit her grave and that then, I said. My grandad had even paid for a plot for her in town. I'd known about that for years. She would have told her bloke about that, I was sure, but he went right ahead and buried her up there in Scotland. I was going to get in touch with my sister at some point. There was a legal thing involved, there were certain rights due to being next of kin. I was going to apply for her to be like transferred or something, once I'd spoken to my sister about it. She had a plot waiting for her in town here. She wasn't supposed to be all the way up there where nobody knew her besides that bloke.

Ray thought it was funny. The idea of moving someone like that, once they were dead. The idea of anyone giving a shit where they were buried once they were dead, was what he said. What he said as well was he'd buy me a shovel himself. That was when I told him to shut up. He said I will I'll buy you a shovel. I said Ray, leave it. He said don't worry about fucking legal process, I'll buy you a shovel and you can dig up your mam. I said Ray fucking leave it, and I put him on his back and he stopped laughing then.

One thing I remember about Ray's mum. I don't remember much but there's this. When we were kids. We all called round to his house one day and when he opened the front door we heard his mum going Ray will you close the bloody door will you, and when we looked up there she was in the bathroom at the top of the stairs with the door wide open, sat on the throne with everything round her ankles. The bathroom door wide open, and now the front door. And Ray just stood there talking to us and ignoring her while she went Ray! Ray! Will you close the bloody door there Ray! The door! And all of us trying not to look but we must have looked at least once because later we'd all agreed that you could see her bone china and everything. And Ray just kept us there talking for as long as he could before he put his jacket on and came out and left the front door wide open so we could hear her calling after him as we walked away. Ray! Will you get back here and close this bloody door Ray! And the thing we all noticed but nobody said was that it was the exact same voice she used when she called him in for his tea, or just whenever we'd heard her speaking to him at all.

*

It was Ray's car but he mostly let me do the driving. He said the angle of the pedals made his bad back flare up, but also it was because he had trouble concentrating. Plus the blackouts. It was a very particular type of car. It had taken some getting used to. It took a while even getting it started. Also the foot-brake didn't really work properly so I mostly had to rely on the handbrake. Which was another reason I drove so slowly on the way over to the Stewart place that night. We drove right round the back of the marquee and parked up by the catering tent. The catering vans weren't there.

They won't be back until the morning, Ray says. Like he knew. Like he'd been casing the joint or anything. We sat there for a while with the engine running, figuring things out. We could see the portable toilets off to one side of the marquee, and people standing around talking. There was a big flood-light over the toilet, meaning we could see them and they couldn't see us. There was a lot of cheering whenever a new song came on, which meant it was probably only the young ones left in there and the old or sober ones had gone home.

Someone knocked on the window. He had a look of the Stewarts about him. Big square chin and red face and floppy hair. Ray wound down the window. The younger Stewart asked us if we were okay. He was smoking a cigar, or at least he was holding a cigar and wondering what to do with it. Ray looked at him.

Was everything okay with your food? Ray says. The younger Stewart looked confused. He asked us if we were with the caterers. I told him we were just picking up a few things that couldn't be left overnight. He nodded and told us that was a good idea. He turned away and turned back and told us the food had been bloody lovely. We waited until he'd gone back round the corner with his cigar. Ray got out of the car.

Keep the engine running, he says. I think this was meant to sound dramatic but it was obvious and he didn't need to say it. If I'd turned the engine off we wouldn't have got it started again until the next day.

Keep the engine running, he says again. I don't know why he had to say it twice.

*

We must have got about fifty yards back from the can and we were nowhere near knocking it down any more and Ray was still on with his story about writing the porno story. He said he'd just been getting to the best bit when he noticed that the student or schoolgirl or whoever was standing next to his seat. He said he didn't really know how long she'd been standing there. She asked him did she know him or like had she met him before, and he didn't really know what she was getting at so he just said no, sorry, he didn't think she'd met him anywhere.

Then Ray got up and more or less started acting it out, which I could have done without. I just sat there looking at the lake, holding my can, waiting for him to get on with it. He stood there next to me, closer than I could have done with bearing in mind the facilities available to us at the caravan. He had his hand on his hip, meaning I suppose that's how he thought girls always stood when they were talking to you, and he put on this voice which must have been his idea of a girl's voice but sounded more like a cat or something. He said, in this voice, with his hand on his hip, that I kept looking at him like I knew him or something and it was making him like uncomfortable and he would rather I didn't. The way he said it, there was a question mark at the end of each sentence. Also, the way he said it, it sounded like he was about to slap me round the face. He sat down again, as Ray.

244

I could have done without him acting it out but I knew what he was on about. The way these girls are so self-assertive nowadays. They must teach it them at school. Ray wouldn't have been looking at her like that, like the way she said. But there wouldn't have been anything he could say about it. He would have had to just keep his mouth shut and look at the floor. That's what they do. They get you like that. Wouldn't mind being a bit self-assertive like that myself, sometimes. Certain situations it would have helped. I asked Ray what he did after that and he said what did I think he'd done he'd got off the train at the next stop.

These birds all went over then. Geese or something. We could hear their wings going. I still hadn't hit the can from that distance, so I shuffled my chair forward a bit when Ray wasn't looking. It didn't seem like it was getting dark but the lights had gone on in Jackie's house. I said maybe it was time to light a fire. I said it was Ray's turn to get the wood. He said it was my turn. I got the last of the pallets and broke them up with a crowbar and heaped them up in the usual place. Some more of those birds went over and when I looked up I noticed the sky was going out at the edges. I hadn't noticed the sun going down. I went and got some lighter fluid from the caravan and lit the fire. We could see Jackie standing at her bedroom window looking over at the Stewart place. We could hear the kids at one of the houses by the church going on their trampoline. Heard it most nights. Someone should take some light oil to the springs. I sat down again and told Ray that when my daughter was little she'd always called them jumpolines. He asked when the fuck I'd had a daughter. I told him I wasn't going to go into it. He got up to go to the caravan, and I said if he kept polishing his crockery like that it was going to get chipped or something. He didn't think that was funny. He came over and put me off the chair and drew blood from my nose and then he went in the caravan and turned the radio on in there. Thing with Ray is he's one of those people who can drink as much as they want without causing any problems. It's when the drink runs out is when you want to watch him.

Later he told me how the story had ended. Like I'd been hanging on waiting for the final instalment. He said he'd sat on that station platform waiting for the next train and he'd written it right to the end and put it in the post to her. He said it ended with the woman in the story pulling off her blindfold and realising the other people in the story had gone. I said you can leave it there if you like Ray. I was still holding my T-shirt up to my nose to stop the bleeding. He said so this woman could hear them dressing in the other room and going out through the front door, and she wanted to get up or call them back but she was too done in to move or talk or anything, and then she heard the door close and she was all cold and wrapping the sheets round herself and it was getting dark and everything. He said it was something like that anyway. He said it had all been a while ago. He said he'd put it in the post to his ex-wife but he never found out if she got it or not. I asked him what he expected me to say to all that.

He said could I hear that lot, meaning the guests at the Stewart place, meaning they sounded well into it by then. We sat there and listened, looking into the fire. The pallet-wood kept cracking and spitting and all these shrieks of laughter kept coming across the fields.

Fuck it, he said. Let's go.

*

He came walking out of the catering tent with a case of Stella. Just like that, jackpot. He opened the back door and slid it in and I told him nice one Ray let's get going.

Wait there, he says.

He shut the door and went back into the catering tent. I could see the shadow of him moving around in there. Also I could see the younger Stewart standing in the light outside the toilet talking to some people, waving that cigar around but apparently still not smoking it. The air was cold and there were these little wafts of steam rising off him into the light, like the way steam comes off of cows first thing in the morning. The back door opened and Ray dumped what sounded like a case of wine bottles in there. I said Ray you don't even like wine let's just get going.

Wait there you, he says. Give me a few more minutes, he says.

When he eventually came out and got in the car he was carrying some kind of black satchel and a vase of flowers. He told me to drive. He shifted in his seat. He wiped his mouth with the back of his hand. I looked at him. I asked him what he'd been doing in there. He held up the vase. These are for Jackie, he says. I asked him what he'd been doing. He wiped his mouth again and told me to drive.

247

The younger Stewart gave us a wave on our way out. Ray waved back. There were groups of people standing around all along the track out to the road, but no one else looked at us. I drove with the lights off. There was still some light in the sky out to the west, and the moon was high. If it wasn't for the green algae the moon would have been like glinting off the lake when we got back to the caravan. The fire was still burning, just about. The lights were all out at Jackie's house. Ray set the vase of flowers on a flat stone by the lake and ripped open the case of beers. I put the last of the wood on the fire and pulled my chair up close to it and we both opened a beer. I didn't really feel like a drink after all that. I felt like going to bed. Ray put the satchel on his lap and started going through it. He looked like a woman with a handbag. I didn't say that. The blood on my shirt was still wet from before. I threw a stone in the lake. I asked Ray how come the fuck he'd taken a bag for. I told him we'd said just the drinks. I told him it weren't like anyone was going to have to look far before they thought of us. He said to stop whining like a little girl. We couldn't hear much from the Stewart place. They must have been winding down.

I asked Ray what he'd got. He said there was some money but it was all foreign shit it was mostly euros. He said there was a phone with a camera on it. I threw another stone in the lake and finished the beer. I asked him what he was going to do with the euros and he said he was going to go on a day trip to fucking Calais what did I think he was going to do with the euros. He threw a stone at the lake and it hit the vase and the vase fell over without breaking. A couple of Tornadoes went over and dropped bombs on the Sands, and by the time we heard them they must have been long gone. A light went on in Jackie's bedroom. Three more of them went over, and we heard someone screaming or laughing at the Stewart place. Ray said they weren't messing around any more, it was all going to kick off any day now for definite. The light went out in Jackie's bedroom. Ray found a passport in the bag. I told him he could get good money for a passport, I knew someone. He flicked through it. It's from Norway, he said. This is Norwegian shit. Hence why the euros, I started to say, but he stood up and threw the passport and the money on the fire and threw the bag towards the lake. It fell short. I looked at him. I tried to grab the passport out of the fire, but he kicked my hand and told me to leave it the bloody hell well alone. I opened another beer and sat down. I said Ray they're going to come looking for that passport and the rest of the shit. He gave me a look. I shut up and drank my beer. I'd been getting to quite like the caravan and the lake and everything. Another Tornado went over. Looked like we weren't going to get that ditch dug after all. I started asking him what he'd done that for, but he told me to just fucking well leave it.

Don't even get me started on the Norwegians, he says.

Memorial Stone

Tathwell, Cadwell, Burwell, Rothwell, Hemswell, Harpswell, Hemswell Cliff, Cromwell, Upwell, Cranwell, Outwell, Holwell, Ashwell, Maidenwell.

Haltham, Metheringham, Nettleham, Reepham, Welham, Askham, Markham Moor, North Hykeham, Low Marnham, Helpringham, South Witham, High Marnham, New Boultham, Sempringham, Low Burnham, Alvingham, South Willingham, Cherry Willingham, North Willingham, Hagworthingham, Walkeringham, Hykeham Moor, Threekingham, Stokeham, Laneham, Grantham, Wymondham, Haugham, Castle Bytham, Burringham, Messingham, Waddingham, Grayingham, Pilham, Beckingham, Little Bytham, Corringham, Fillingham, Ingham, Cammeringham, Cottam, Dunham, Boultham, Hykeham, Bassingham, Leasingham, Sandringham, Hougham, Cotham, Snettisham, Holdingham, Shouldham Thorpe.

Sandy Bank, Lade Bank, Ten Mile Bank, Wrangle Bank.

Little Steeping, Great Steeping.

Willoughton, Blyton, Doddington, Burton, Toft next Newton, Newton by Toft, Misterton, Morton, Rampton, Laughton, Laughterton, Welton, Gosberton Clough, Scampton, Scotton, Screveton, Shelton, Sapperton, Syston, Aslockton, Marston, Ruskington, Dorrington, Heckington, Quarrington, Ossington, Orston, Carlton Scroop, North Carlton, South Carlton, South Clifton, East Drayton, Gate Burton, High Toynton, Low Langton, Wold Newton, North Reston, South Reston, Carlton on Trent, Holton cum Beckering, Sturton le Steeple, Kirton in Lindsey, Thornton le Moor, Carlton-le-Moorland, Keddington Corner, North Leverton with Habblesthorpe, Newton on Trent, Bishop Norton, Norton Disney, Market Stainton, Toynton Fen Side, Burton Coggles, Burton Pedwardine, Burton Lazars, Normanton, Haddington, Honington, Allington, Branston, Barkston, Wyberton West, South Leverton, Dry Doddington, Stewton Keddington, East Torrington, Market Overton, North Elkington, South Elkington, Kirton Holme, West Torrington, South Cockerington, North Cockerington, Croxton Kerrial, East Heckington, Halton Fenside, Langton by Wragby, Sutton on Trent, Sproxton, Skillington, Creeton, Baston, Stretton, Thistleton, Moulton, Etton, Bainton, Ashton, Helpston, Upton, Fenton, Darlton, Gelston, Thoroton, Alverton, Stroxton, Muston, Foston, Scredington, Denton, Knipton, Harston, Donington, Drayton, Freiston, Leverton, Benington, Horsington, Holton le Moor, Moortown, Muckton, Gayton, Sutterton, Hainton,

Harrington, Donington on Bain, Harlaxton, Hungerton, Hallington, Luddington, Spridlington, Lissington, Welton le Wold, Leverington, Frampton, Kirton, Asperton, Gosberton, Pointon, Langton, Thornton, Elton, Belton, Newton, Nocton, Halton Holegate, Wyberton East, Kirmington, Edlington, Wispington, Fiskerton, Long Bennington, Low Toynton, Low Stanton, Little Carlton, Little Welton, Little Ponton, Woolton, Broughton, Dunston, Langton, Sutton, Swaton, Eaton, Croxton, Coston, Kirton End, Great Ponton, Lenton, Panton, Heighington, Great Carlton, Nettleton, Normanton on Trent.

Scrafield, Stainfield, Bitchfield, Kelfield, Gorefield.

Wildsworth, Hawksworth, Pickworth, Colsterworth, Stainton by Langworth, Potterhanworth, Cold Hanworth, Faldingworth, Tamworth Green, West Barkwith, East Barkwith, Benniworth, Butterwick, Susworth, West Stockwith, Ailsworth, East Stockwith, Epworth, Langworth, Epworth Turbary.

Ticks Moor, West Moor.

Gayton le Marsh, Chapel Six Marshes, Marshchapel, Holbeach Marsh.

Brentingby, Wyfordby, Bescaby, Stonesby, Saxby, Stainby, Gunby, Dunsby, Hacconby, Ingoldsby, Keisby, Dalderby, Winceby, Asgarby, Hundleby, Scrivelsby, Spilsby, New Spilsby, Great Dalby, South Ormsby, Wood Enderby, Ab Kettleby, Old Somerby, Bag Enderby, Coningsby, Miningsby,

Aslackby, Hanby, Humby, Thimbleby, Gautby, Wickenby, Fulnetby, Bleasby, Wragby, Sotby, Ranby, Goulceby, Asterby, Raithby, Maltby, Scamblesby, Swaby, Grimoldby, Manby, Aunby, Careby, Carlby, Thrulby, Saltby, Revesby, Raithby, Dalby, Graby, Dowsby, Tumby, Thoresby, Somersby, Goadby Marwood, Kirkby Green, Boothby Pagnell, Kirkby on Bain, Ashby Puerorum, Irby in the Marsh, Hemingby, Tealby, Kirkby, Kingerby, Ketsby, Calceby, Rigsby, Raithby, Sutterby, Utterby, Ashby de la Lounde, North Ormsby, North Thoresby, Grimsby, Tumby Woodside, Mavis Enderby, New Spilsby, West Ashby, Little Dalby, Little Grimsby, Ashby cum Fenby, Normanby le Wold, Fulletby, Salmonby, Worlaby, Fotherby, Legsby, Walesby, Osgodby, Usselby, Claxby, Croxby, Grainsby, Hagnaby, Aylesby, Candlesby, Barnoldby le Beck, Irby upon Humber, Ulceby Skitter, Dragonby, Keadby, Ulceby Cross, Ulceby, Worlaby, Bonby, Wrawby, Appleby, Risby, Brumby, Scawby, Bigby, Somerby, Searby, Owmby, Grasby, Clixby, Usselby, Snitterby, Atterby, Aisby, Saundby, Kexby, Normanby, Saxby, Barnetby le Wold, Hareby, Wilksby, Brattleby, Bransby, Skegby, Harby, Saxilby, Whisby, Thurlby, Firsby, Boothby Graffoe, Navenby, Digby, Ewerby, Asgarby, North Rauceby, South Rauceby, East Kirkby, East Firsby, Aisby, Aunsby, West Firsby, Gonerby Hill Foot, Grebby, Aswardby, Driby, Osbournby, Caenby, Granby, Barrowby, Welby, Oasby, Kelby, Braceby, Haceby, Dembleby, Aswarby, Scott Willoughby, Silk Willoughby, Saltfleetby, Great Gonerby, North Owersby, South Owersby, Spanby, Coleby, Ashby, Aby.

Westry, Whittlesey, March.

Dogsthorpe, Longthorpe, Westhorpe, Wilsthorpe, Belmesthorpe, Northorpe, Obthorpe, Manthorpe, Leesthorpe, Grimsthorpe, Elsthorpe, Scottlethorpe, Hawthorpe, Hanthorpe, Garthorpe, Milthorpe, Castlethorpe, Kettlethorpe, Skellingthorpe, Grassthorpe, Besthorpe, Winthorpe, Kirkby la Thorpe, Woolsthorpe by Colsterworth, Woolsthorpe, Derrythorpe, Birthorpe, Far Thorpe, Mid Thorpe, Kingthorpe, Swinthorpe, Friesthorpe, Woodthorpe, Claythorpe, Authorpe, Althorpe, Yaddlethorpe, Yawthorpe, Thorpe in the Fallows, Caythorpe, Sibthorpe, Biscathorpe, Buslingthorpe, Scunthorpe, Grainthorpe, Londonthorpe, Scotterthorpe, Northorpe, Gunthorpe, Springthorpe, Culverthorpe, Mablethorpe, Manthorpe, Aisthorpe, Hogsthorpe, Little Cawthorpe, Trusthorpe, Thorpe Satchville, Thorpe Arnold, Thorpe.

Loosegate, Fleet Hargate, Gate Burton, Broadgate, Horsegate, Halesgate, Wrangle Lowgate, Deeping Gate, Westgate, Chapelgate, Guanockgate, Halton Holegate, Gedney Broadgate.

Dogdyke, Skeldyke, Seadyke, Fosdyke, Austendike, Gedney Dyke, Thorpe Fendykes, Quadring Eaudike, Dyke.

Old Leake, Leake Commonside, Leake Gride, New Leake, Leake Ings.

Pinchbeck, Pinchbeck Bars, Swallowbeck, Pinchbeck West, Fulbeck, Woodbeck, Sudbrooke, Binbrook, Sedgebrook.

Chainbridge, Cuckoo Bridge, Fosdyke Bridge, Swineshead Bridge, Hubbert's Bridge, Gipsey Bridge, Bishopbridge, Bracebridge, Friday Bridge, Pondersbridge, Tattershall Bridge, Forty Foot Bridge.

Stickford, Tetford, Belchford, Snarford, Ludford, Spalford, Stapleford, Langford, Sleaford, Hazelford, Bottesford, Scalford, Twyford, Greatford.

Owston Ferry, East Ferry, High Ferry.

Holbeach St Matthew, Holbeach St Marks, Holbeach St Johns, Marshland St James, Sutton St James, Sutton St Edmund, Deeping St James, Deeping St Nicholas, Wisbech St Mary, Wainfleet St Mary, Witham St Hughs, Saltfleetby St Peter, Toynton St Peter, Thorpe St Peter, Walpole St Peter, Walpole St Andrew, Terrington St John, Tilney St Lawrence, Theddlethorpe St Helen, Wiggenhall St Germans, Wiggenhall St Mary the Virgin, Wiggenhall St Mary Magdalen, Toynton All Saints, Saxby All Saints, Wainfleet All Saints, Theddlethorpe All Saints.

Ring's End, Fen End, Surfeet Seas End, Tongue End, Brand End, Moulton Seas End, Scrane End, Kirton End, Frampton West End, Fishmere End, North End, Benington Sea End, Halltoft End, Ashington End, Gedney Drove End, Tilney High End, Bridge End, Castle End, Church End.

Eastville, Midville, Wyville, Frithville, Little London, Jerusalem, Gibraltar, Boston, New England, Newark, New York.

Acknowledgments

'In Winter The Sky' was first published, in a different form and under the title of 'What The Sky Sees', in *Granta* 78, 2002.

'If It Keeps On Raining' was first published in the BBC National Short Story Award 2010 anthology, by Comma Press. It was also broadcast on Radio 4 in November 2010.

The title of 'Fleeing Complexity' is taken from an interview with Richard Ford conducted by Tim Adams, published in *Granta* 99, 2007.

'Which Reminded Her, Later' was first published in *Granta* 99, 2007.

'Close' was commissioned by the Cheltenham Literary Festival, and first broadcast on Radio 4 in October 2007. It was first published in *The Sea of Azov*, a World Jewish Relief anthology published by Five Leaves, 2009.

'We Wave And Call' was first published by the *Guardian* Weekend magazine in 2011.

'Supplementary Notes To The Testimony' was inspired by stories I was told whilst on a trip to the Nuba Mountains of Sudan, and uses the very broadly transposed outlines of those stories as its unseen background. Many thanks to Carbino, Anil Osman and Mahamud Ismail for speaking so openly with me; and thanks to Médecins Sans Frontières and the *Sunday Times* for organising and supporting the trip. I also drew on an interview with Mark Argent, a demining engineer working with Danish Churches Aid in the Nuba Mountains (any errors in the section about landmines being my own, of course), and on a 2001 *Observer* article by Burhan Wazir.

'Wires' was first published in the BBC National Short Story Award 2011 anthology, by Comma Press. It was also broadcast on Radio 4 in September 2011.

Thanks, variously, for support, insight, reading and inspiration, to the following: Kathy Belden, Tracy Bohan, Katie Bond, Cassie Browne, Sarah-Jane Forder, Helen Garnons-Williams, Peter Gustavsson, Pippa Hennesey, Chloe Hooper, Erica Jarnes, Maggie and David Jones, Anne Joseph, Kirstie Joynson, Tam Laniado, Elena Lappin, Éireann Lorsung, Carrie Majer, Colum McCann, Maile Meloy, Nottingham Writers' Studio, Richard Pilgrim, Mark Robson, the Society of Authors, Craig Taylor, Matthew Welton, Oliver Wood, Writing East Midlands, John Young.

And thanks, for everything, to Alice, Eleanor and Lewis.

IF NOBODY SPEAKS OF REMARKABLE THINGS

On a street in a town in the north of England, ordinary people are going through the motions of their everyday existence – street cricket, barbecues, painting windows... A young man is in love with a neighbour who does not even know his name. An old couple make their way up to the nearby bus stop. But then a terrible event shatters the quiet of the early summer evening. That this remarkable and horrific event is only poignant to those who saw it, not even meriting a mention on the local news, means that those who witness it will be altered for ever.

'A dream of a novel'
ERICA WAGNER, THE TIMES

'You won't read anything much more poignant than this'
WILLIAM LEITH, DAILY TELEGRAPH

SO MANY WAYS TO BEGIN

David Carter cannot help but wish for more: that his wife Eleanor would be the sparkling girl he once found so irresistible; that his job as a museum curator could live up to the promise it once held; that his daughter's arrival could have brought him closer to Eleanor. But a few careless words spoken by his mother's friend have left David restless with the knowledge that his whole life has been constructed around a lie.

'An homage to ordinary people and ordinary things, to the parts of our lives that often go unspoken ... moving and honest'
THE TIMES

'An intimate tale with penetrating things to say about the wider history of twentieth-century Britain'
SUNDAY TIMES

BLOOMSBURY

EVEN THE DOGS

On a still, freezing day between Christmas and New Year, a man's body is found lying in his ruined flat. In the gritty days that follow, those who knew him recreate his neglected life and look on as his body is examined, investigated and cremated. And as they watch, their own stories unfurl layer by layer; stories of hopes flaring and dying and of lives fallen through the cracks. Shockingly powerful and intensely moving, *Even the Dogs* is an intimate portrayal of existence from beyond the comfort zone.

'Jon McGregor treads with unflinching respect through the debris of this dead man's home ... *Even the Dogs* is a short, brilliant and beautiful lesson in empathy'
DAILY MAIL

'Unmissable … McGregor's prose is unflinching yet luminous'
GUARDIAN

'Set in a desolate urban winter landscape, this is a powerful portrait of homelessness, violence and despair on the fringes of society ****'
MAIL ON SUNDAY

ORDER BY PHONE: +44 (0)1256 302 699; BY EMAIL: DIRECT@MACMILLAN.CO.UK

DELIVERY IS USUALLY 3–5 WORKING DAYS. POSTAGE AND PACKAGING WILL BE CHARGED.

ONLINE: WWW.BLOOMSBURY.COM/BOOKSHOP

FREE POSTAGE AND PACKAGING FOR ORDERS OVER £20.

PRICES AND AVAILABILITY SUBJECT TO CHANGE WITHOUT NOTICE.

WWW.BLOOMSBURY.COM/JONMCGREGOR

B L O O M S B U R Y